The next book can't come fast enough. – *Sarita*

Highly recommend this exciting time-traveling saga with romance, mystery, and suspense. You won't want to miss this continuation of the story. – *Kim*

No Unturned Stone shows what happens when powerhouses, Susan May Warren and James Rubart team up with David Warren to give us some of the best storytelling I have read in a very long time. – *Jessica H.*

Oh my word! Where do I even begin? Love suspense? Read this book. Love time travel? Read this book. Love to have the unexpected happen? Read this book. Love going through the ups and downs with the characters? You know what I'm going to say, right? – *Mimi*

So much happens in this book that you'll be on the edge of your seat during your whole read – which will be quick, because you won't be able to put it down! – *Amy B.*

This book and series is just full of all the feels. It's intense, with an intriguing plot and great characters. Definitely recommended! – *Tressa*

If you enjoy suspense, murder mysteries, romance, and a small dose of speculative fiction grab this book and series and don't look back! – *Meagan*

The Rembrandt Stone books are a fascinating mix of the genres of detective/ police procedural/time travel, woven together to create the most exciting suspense thriller I've read in ages! Don't miss this incredible book. You'll be in for a rollercoaster ride! – *Wren*

Oh. My. Gosh. I have no words to describe this novel, other than the fact that it was incredible. Seriously, everyone who loves mysteries needs to read this book! I thought I liked the first one of the series, but that was nothing compared to this wild ride! – *Beth*

THE TRUE LIES
OF REMBRANDT STONE

STICKS AND STONE

TriStone Media Group
Minneapolis, MN

Tristone Media Inc.

15100 Mckenzie Blvd

Minnetonka, Minnesota, 55345

Copyright © 2021 by Tristone Media

ISBN: 978-1-954023-05-5

www.RembrandtStone.com

SOLI DEO GLORIA

CHAPTER 1

The pieces of two lives sit in my brain like they should fit together, but no matter how hard I press, I can't get them to line up.

My life is broken into fragments that refuse to align.

All I know is that some mistakes you can never escape, no matter how you try.

And believe me, I've tried.

I'm standing on the muddy shoreline in the shadow of the Stone Arch Bridge on the east bank of the Mississippi River. The morning sun is low, just brimming the horizon, gilding the water a deep, fire-orange, and turning the skyline of Minneapolis a brilliant gold. I'm watching my crime scene investigators tape off a wooded area of the Historic Main Street Park just off Anthony and Main.

A woman's naked body is covered, awaiting the CSI director—my former wife, although she has no memory of that—and the coroner is on his way.

I'm nursing my second cup of coffee, the first one downed this morning at o-dark hundred as I crawled out of bed to the text of my assistant, Inspector Zeke Kincaid.

My head is fuzzy because, as I said, I'm trying to fit together pieces that aren't made for this puzzle.

This puzzle belongs to Rembrandt Stone, Bureau Chief Inspector for the Minneapolis Police Department and head of the task force overseeing the Jackson serial killings.

I am Rembrandt Stone, former investigator turned failed novelist, father to a seven-year-old daughter, gone missing in time, husband to a wife who can't remember being married to him, and the owner of a time-traveling watch.

This is a lifetime I haven't yet lived, and although the pieces are starting to form, I'm going to need a lot more coffee.

And help.

Here's what I know—and you'd better write this down because I'm getting some of my facts mixed up as time folds upon itself.

Four days ago, while I was celebrating my daughter's seventh birthday with my beautiful wife Eve, a box of cold case files was delivered along with an old broken watch, gifts bequeathed to me by Police Chief John Booker after his death.

Three days ago, I took said watch to a repairman who told me it was working just fine. Maybe it was, because as I looked over my cold cases—specifically the first one involving the bombing of three coffee shops over twenty-three years ago—I inadvertently wound the watch.

And ended up at the scene of the first bombing.

Back in time.

I know what you're thinking—me too. Maybe I'd had too much Macallan whiskey for a night cap. But stay with me—I solved those bombings and prevented the third. And woke up in a new reality. One where my wife stood on my doorstep and handed me divorce papers.

One where Ashley had been murdered, two years before.

One I desperately needed to escape.

So, *two* days ago, I sought out the watchmaker, and he—and his daughter—suggested I'd overwritten the events of my previous timeline.

Intending to rewrite them yet again, yesterday, I traveled back to my second cold case, one involving a young woman murdered near a diner. I'll be honest—my goal wasn't to solve her crime, but to stop another…the drive-by shooting deaths of Eve's father and brother.

Really, it's not that hard to change history when you know the time and place history is going to happen. Danny and Asher lived. Unfortunately, Eve's mother, Bets, was shot in the crossfire and I was sucked back to the present before I knew whether she lived or not.

Yesterday, when I returned to *this* reality, I found Eve married to my partner, Burke.

Former partner Burke. I'm still figuring out that glitch.

And dealing what feels like a serious gut punch.

And, worse, Ashley doesn't exist in this timeline. Has *never* existed.

Are you keeping up?

Maybe we should simply rewind time to yesterday when I arrived back—or should I say forward?—to now, and discovered, as bad as it is, my life isn't in complete tatters.

I'm not a drunk, I'm not on the verge of divorce, my daughter isn't among the victims, strangled in her pajamas, torn from our lives as she slept in her upstairs bedroom.

On the contrary, I'm successful. Published.

And I still have my Porsche.

I have an okay life.

It's just not a life I want. In fact, without Eve and Ashley...

My house is the same—the 1930s Craftsman, off Drew

Avenue, close enough to the lakes for us—me—to feel like we're near a park, but with the skyline of Minneapolis just a stone's throw away.

My house hasn't been remodeled, and that's probably because I no longer have Eve in my ear, drawing out her dreams on graph paper. Inside, my office bookcase is filled with a row of bestsellers, my name on the spine, so now I know what I do on my nights off.

I share the house with Asher Mulligan, Eve's kid brother. Or at least he was twenty years ago. I nearly tackled him as he came in the door, mostly because I didn't recognize him, having never known Asher as an adult. Because, you know, he died. Until he didn't.

Oh boy.

He's apparently my roommate, a white-hat hacker and someone with whom I'm friendly, if not close.

I don't know who I'm close to, really, because the only two people in my life I'd put in that category have each other now.

Eve, my wife, and Burke.

Andrew Burke, my former partner. Who now hates me and bears a terrible burn scar across his face. I'm going to get to the bottom of that.

My office is still a conference room, but now, instead of twenty-three horrific murders, thirty-eight cases line the board.

Thirty-eight women killed by a man we—*I?*—have dubbed the Jackson killer, because of his calling card, a twenty-dollar bill.

What no one knows is that inscribed on each twenty are the words, "thank you for your service."

Sick.

The only anomaly in the lineup of cases is still the murder of my old boss, John Booker.

My daughter's case, however, is absent, because, like I said, she doesn't exist.

Never existed.

See why I need to write things down? Because I sound a little crazy when I say it out loud.

"Rem. I thought I'd find you here."

The voice turns me and just like always I'm blown over by the sight of Eve walking onto a crime scene.

Her auburn hair is tied back, and she's wearing a pair of hiking boots, jeans and her CSI vest. And, she's just as beautiful as she was yesterday, or the day before and twenty-three years ago when I kissed her on the steps of her home.

She's not mine. And she probably just rolled out of the bed she shares with Burke and I need to not let that find root in my brain if I hope to survive in this world.

Time is cruel. Or maybe it's fate. I'm not sure, but frankly, Eve belongs to me. And I know that sounds rather Neanderthal, but that's just where I am right now.

I'm not sure why the idea of her, happy, with my best friend is worse than her divorcing me. I just can't believe she moved on after what we had. Or maybe we, like Ash, never existed because Eve looks at me with a friendly smile, nothing of a spark in her eyes, and my throat thickens.

I probably need more coffee.

No, I need to rewind time, rescue my old life, and throw the watch into the Mississippi.

She is carrying a pair of gloves, but she doesn't do the heavy lifting anymore. Not as director of the crime lab.

She stands at the edge of the crime scene and stares at the body. "What do we know?"

This information is recent, handed to me by Zeke. "Female, early twenties. From the marks at her neck, she was strangled. She's naked, but in her hand is—"

"A twenty-dollar bill."

"Yeah."

"Is it marked?"

"Yes," I say and finish off my coffee.

"I hope we can get some DNA off her."

"Maybe, hopefully, she fought him," I say. "Look under her fingernails."

Eve gives me a look. "We'll get him, Rem," she says. "By the way, why did you want me to pull the DNA off the Delany case?"

I stare at her, a coil tightening around my chest.

The Delany case?

Eve is snapping on her gloves. "Although, admittedly, I realized we didn't pull DNA the first time, so it's a good thing. I'm running the match through the CODIS database just to see if we get a hit on Fitzgerald."

That's right. Lauren Delany. The working girl killed outside Sonny's Bar. She had a twenty in her pocket. Did I identify her as a Jackson murder? The first go-round, she was just an unlucky girl who'd been picked up by the wrong John.

Until now, that John was unnamed. But now, it's Leo Fitzgerald. The name is a recent acquisition to my memory, and it takes me just a moment to nail it. Leo Fitzgerald, the lead suspect in the Jackson murders. Former military, bomb-maker and the man whose explosive ambush killed John Booker.

He's been in the wind for three years.

He's been the primary suspect since his DNA was found on his dead girlfriend, Gretchen Anderson, who was strangled, sexually assaulted and marked with the first of the Jackson bills. But that doesn't happen for two more years...or rather two years after Lauren Delany's case.

So what was I thinking? And by *I*, I mean the Rem who

occupied this body in the timeline I jumped into. He asked Eve to dig up the old case and run the DNA tests.

I hope he's onto something.

Eve starts down the hill toward the activity, but I can't help myself. "Hey—how's your mom?"

She looks up at me. "She's good, Rem, thanks. But you just saw her two days ago at my dad's memorial party." She frowns.

The Danny Mulligan Annual Birthday Party, the precinct-wide bash Bets has every year to celebrate her husband's life, even in death. So, I'm still invited to that? "Right. Yeah, I just…I don't know." Two days ago, she lay bleeding in the sidewalk of Eve's childhood home. *Catch up, Rem!*

I need a time travel assistant, someone who reminds me where I am, and why. But the right words form in my soul. "It's just been a long time since Danny's death, and I…you just don't get over losing someone you love, right?"

She gives me a smile, and it's sweet. "Sometimes, Rem, you remind me of a guy I used to know." She winks then and heads down the hill.

I can't breathe.

It was real. What we had. I saw it flash in her eyes—me, holding her in my arms, she, smiling up at me a second before she kisses me.

It was absolutely, no question, we-were-made-for-each other real.

So, then…It's me. *I'm* the reason we're not together. I'm the one who colossally screwed up.

My heart seizes. I need to sit down—

"Boss, we found some clothes." The words from Zeke shake me out of the spiral of despair and back to the investigation. "It looks like a T-shirt."

Zeke is young, maybe mid-twenties, with a man bun and built like a guy who works out after hours. He sort of reminds me of me, back when I lived for this job. He's wearing a pair of dress pants, an untucked striped shirt, his sleeves rolled up, and purple evidence gloves. I really don't know much about him, but I like him. He's eager. And right now, he's the closest thing to a friend that I have, so I'm on him like Velcro.

Someone, anyone, needs to point me in the right direction.

Zeke is directing one of the CSIs to take a picture of the evidence he's pointing to.

I take a breath, give one glance back at Eve, walk over and crouch next to him as he holds up the underbrush around the shirt. "What, the killer tosses this away as he's fleeing?"

"Or maybe during the crime, and he didn't have the time to find it?"

Zeke holds the shirt up. "Pillsbury Diner. It's a place just across the street. Great burgers, live music."

I know the place, and the thought sends a strange heat through me. A conversation is forming in the back of my head. I can't quite make it out, but I will, give me, ahem, time. "Turn it over."

Again, I'm not sure why, but something in my gut just knows...

He turns the shirt over.

Great. I puff out a quick sigh

A footprint.

I know I'm cheating, because I remember now a victim from a different time, laying in a hospital bed... *"It happened so fast. I was coming out of work at Pillsbury's and I heard someone behind me. I started running, and he tackled me. He put his foot in my back and held me down...*

I'm scrambling for her name, but it's buried under layers of other memories.

"I wonder how she got here," Zeke says.

"He surprised her after work, as she was coming out into the parking lot." It's not a hunch—I'm remembering my bedside conversation with the victim. Her name...her *name*. It's lodged in the back of my brain.

But deep inside, I hope I'm wrong. That this woman is not the blonde I met in the hospital, the only daughter of a couple from the suburbs. "She probably ran, and he caught up to her." I gesture to the footprint. "He held her down."

"We'll get this tread into the database and see what we can find." Zeke bags the evidence.

I walk over to the edge of the yellow tape, duck under it and hike down to the crime scene. Eve is looking at the body, the strangulation marks at her neck, the evidence of assault. She picks up the girl's hands. "She chews her nails. Nothing to grab skin," she says. "And the DNA might be washed away. It looks like her body might have been pushed into the water, then pulled out."

Her hair is wet and muddy, her lower lip gray, split. My memory flashes, but it's too brief to capture.

"I found her purse!" Zeke shouts. He's standing near a park bench. Eve follows me as we hike up the hill. We wait for the photographer, then I glove up as Eve picks up the purse. It's small, the kind that a woman wears over her shoulder, to her hip. What does Eve call that—a clutch?

"It's a crossbody bag," Eve says as she opens it. "So it's funny that it would have fallen off. Unless she was surprised, and it fell off her shoulder as she ran." She pulls out a small wallet.

I hold my breath. Because I remember now. Hollie Larue. Age twenty-three. Pretty, despite the black eye, the split lip. Her voice is soft, shaky in my head. *He told me not to scream...*

Eve opens the wallet. Tucked inside is her driver's license.

I look away, to the river flowing downstream, past the stone bridge, into the horizon where time is beginning a new day.

And, as she reads the name, I brace myself.

"Her name is Hollie Larue."

Yep.

This death is on me.

CHAPTER 2

I left out a few things about last night. It's not that I don't want to talk about it—it's that, I'm not sure they matter.

I'm not sure that, tomorrow, we won't be juggling a new set of story pieces.

But for now, you should know that apparently, I'm dating. Her name is Shelby Ruthers.

In my memory, she dated Burke for a while. She's pretty— the kind of pretty that can get a guy into trouble. Tall, curvy and blonde, I can see why this me has taken a step in her direction.

In my memory, she worked dispatch after being on patrol for a few years. Tried, but never made, investigator.

In this timeline, she sells pharmaceuticals and has a zippy little Beemer which she parked in my driveway not long after I arrived home to my new world.

I was sitting in my office, reading through the reports of the fire that took Danny's life.

It's a fire I remember—mostly because it's the cold case that haunts Burke. We all have one—the case that burns in our soul and shakes us awake at night. For me, it was the bombings, the over twenty lives lost.

Now, it's starting to be the Jackson murders.

Because, you know, the *math*. The fact that had I not gone back to stop the bombings, none of these women would be dead. None.

And it's occurred to me, that something about stopping that last bombing has ignited the killings.

The victims, who are now not victims, went on to live their lives. Maybe one of them is the killer. Except, the file is no longer among my cold cases, because I solved it.

I was feeling a little less smug about that as I searched through the news clippings about the fire.

It happened November 3rd, right after the first big blizzard of the season in Minneapolis. The house, to my memory, and according to the news, was abandoned, except I now know differently. Located in the Powderhorn Park district, sometimes the homeless took refuge in it on particularly cold nights.

And on this night, it sheltered two runaway children whose mother had just been murdered in front of them. I know because Burke and I were on the case. Fadima Mahad, elementary school aide, refugee from Somalia, gunned down in front of her sister's house in the Standish neighborhood.

We searched for her children for two days before finally finding them at the Powderhorn house. Trapped on the third floor, the house was already an inferno.

Burke tried to get in, but the flames—and I, frankly—forced him away.

The children died, and it hit Burke like a sledge in the chest. I've never known why, but that's how it is with crimes, especially those involving children. They get in your heart like tentacles and latch on, stealing a something from you. Hope, maybe.

So, you can see why I can't let go of Ashley.

Clearly something I did caused Burke to run into that house. And for Danny to be shot.

I was searching through police reports, coming up empty when I heard the car drive up. I looked out the window, expecting to see Asher—

Shelby Ruthers?

I met her at the door, and she put one hand on my chest, pushed me back against the wall and kissed me. Full lips, open mouth.

Just like that.

The kind of kiss that told me we know each other and I froze for a long second, trying to get my feet under me before I took her by the arms and pulled her away.

My heart thundered, and my gut clenched with my betrayal.

I know, I know. Eve is married to someone else. But I'm not. I'm still married to Eve.

She smiled up at me. "Hey, Remy."

Remy?

Now listen, Shelby is pretty. Really pretty, in a sort of blonde Scarlett Johansson way. Same figure. And smart. Good wit. I get why Burke liked her.

I just always thought she was a little too committed to her own personal goals to be a good partner, in life, and on the job.

Honestly, and promise you won't tell anyone, but one of those times she applied for inspector, I was the one who denied her application.

As she smiled at me, my throat thickened and I wondered if she knew. Like, cosmically.

"I just got back from Miami." She unbuttoned her shirt, just one button down, and I was about to grab her hand to stop whatever she had on her mind when she held open her shirt. "Got a tan, see?"

I didn't glance down. "Yep."

"It was glorious. I closed the deal with Mount Sinai's cardiology group, and still had time for a day on the beach." She dropped her satchel in my entry way. "We need a day on the lake. Soon." She took a step back in my arms, her hand on my face. "We should call Eve and Burke and see if they want to take the boat out. Sounds fun, yeah?"

Eve and Burke have a boat?

I grabbed her hand, and slid it off me, a sweat breaking out down my spine. I'm a guy, yes, but I still love my wife.

And she's out there, waiting for me.

And I know that doesn't exactly make sense, but in my head, my life has just been put on a shelf somewhere, and I just need to find the right combination to retrieve it.

There's another theory, one posed to me by the daughter of Arthur Fox, watchmaker and time traveler, a woman named Meggie. She believed my old life is gone, overwritten by my meddling in time and that I need to live with what I get.

Not a chance.

I could tell Shelby wasn't leaving so I picked up her satchel and carried it to the kitchen, asking her if she wanted something to drink—preferably something cool.

I opened my fridge and was again both jolted and surprised by the contents. Vegetables, tofu, and almond milk. And, my cupboard was filled with protein shakes.

And I have the body to show for it—I admit to checking it out; I'm looking good for fifty-two.

I did find a chilled bottle of white wine, half-full and corked on the fridge door. Maybe—

Bingo. I turned to find Shelby holding a wine glass she procured from my cupboard, like she knows the place.

I really don't want to know how well.

I poured her a glass, and circled back to her comment. "Eve and Burke's boat? But I thought. I mean…" And really, I had no one else to ask, so, "Are Burke and I still friends?"

She slid onto a hightop chair at the kitchen bar as she gave me a puzzled look. Only then did I notice that I had upgraded the kitchen—at least with stainless appliances. And in the backyard, near where my giant elm used to sit…I have. A. Boat.

She's a beautiful red and white wake-surfing powerboat, on a trailer, with a surf pipe and a surf gate and my brain just stopped.

Rem, you dog.

I was staring, and Shelby snapped her fingers to break me away. "Remy. What are you talking about? Of course you're friends."

I looked at her because, well, truth is, the last time I saw Burke, just a few hours ago, he looked right at me with so much darkness in his eyes, it felt like a punch to my sternum.

"Are you sure?"

She lifted a shoulder. "Well, Eve and I are friends, so you have to be, right?"

I don't know. How together are we, me and Shelby?

I didn't see any pictures of her in my house. Or clothing…

Wait.

"Shelby, do you live here?"

And I know how that sounds, but I didn't have time to censor my words. Shelby leaned forward, blue eyes shining. "Not officially. Why? Are you asking?"

Oh. Boy. "No…I mean. Uh." And I had nothing. So I simply changed the topic. I'm smart that way. "I keep thinking about Burke. He looked pretty mad at me last time I saw him—"

"Oh, that's just Burke. You know how he is. He's always grumpy."

He is?

"You have to stop being so sensitive. Yes, you got all the breaks, but Burke made his choices. He has to live with them."

What choices? And the words were almost in my throat when the door opened.

I was saved by Asher who came into the kitchen with a box of computer supplies and one of his lackeys. Asher owns an Internet security company—news I found out after he left and I pulled up Google—and as he came in, he took a look at me, and grinned. "Sorry. I don't want to interrupt, but all my bandwidth is being gobbled up at the office. I need to set up camp here." He glanced at the woman helping him set up his computer. "This is Briana. She works with me."

Asher is the brother we named Ashley after, since, well, he died. But seeing him, his brownish red hair a little long, wearing a T-shirt under his suitcoat, a pair of jeans and Cons, I wondered if the cosmos had traded my daughter for him.

I don't know how to feel.

But when Shelby slid off the stool and announced she needed to go—her wine still full in her glass—I could place at least one emotion.

Gratitude.

I saw her to the door, and managed to miss her kiss, letting it land on my cheek. She laughed. "Don't tell me you're working on the Jackson case."

"Yes," I said. "I'll call you tomorrow?"

She blew me a kiss, and I felt a little like a jerk for stealing her *Remy* from her.

I walked out into the kitchen, where Asher was setting up his computer. Briana is cute, petite, brunette and looked at Asher with what appeared to be hero worship. Yikes. Maybe I needed to leave.

"Ash, do you know anything about Burke, well, hating me?"

Asher looked up at me, gave me a frown and laughed. "Well, if you don't count his bachelor party, where you told him that my sister belonged to you, and that he stole her…"

Wow, I did that? "That was thirteen years ago."

He frowned. "Thirteen? Try three."

It was?

Asher shook his head. "Probably he's just mad because you won't let him adopt Daphne. But I don't blame you, right? I wouldn't let another man adopt my daughter either."

You can imagine the explosions that happened in my head.

What?

Asher must have noticed the way I grabbed onto the back of a kitchen chair, maybe even grew pale because he glanced up at me. "Dude, are you okay?"

I don't think I nodded. I'm still not sure what to make of his words.

I have a daughter? In this timeline?

"How did this happen?" I said, like an idiot. And I know— stupid question, really, but…I mean, you saw Eve and Burke together, right? I didn't dream that.

Asher raised an eyebrow. "How—?"

"I don't mean *how*. But how did—" I looked up at him. "How did Eve end up marrying *Burke*?"

"Oh, that." Asher sighed, shook his head. "It's simple, man. You never asked her to marry *you*."

And if I thought I was an idiot before, in the previous time-line, I am blown away at my stupidity in this one.

Yes, it was real. At least to Eve.

Just not to me.

Now, standing at the crime scene twenty-four hours later, I watch Eve tuck away Hollie's license back into her wallet. As she bags the evidence and gets up, she suddenly looks tired. Resigned.

"What makes a man do this?" she says to me, not looking at me. "What makes a man go crazy and kill so many people?"

I have no answers.

The most common reason is anger, and the dark thrill of doing something destructive. Other reasons include the need for attention and a deep-seated compulsion.

Twisted pieces of his soul.

Or maybe it started with despair.

"I don't know," I stand up next to her and watch as they bag the body of Hollie Larue.

"We have to stop him," she says quietly, and looks over at me.

"Yes, we do," I say. But my throat is glue.

Because I can't go back in time.

I can't change this.

Not if it means I'm going to lose another daughter.

CHAPTER 3

I'm disturbed by my own frustrated scribbles.

After the medical examiner took Hollie's body away, I had the unfortunate job of calling Deborah and Nate Larue to deliver the devastating news.

That always puts a fist into my gut, tears away my appetite and makes me want to throw a few punches down at Quincy's, the boxing gym where Burke and I used to meet after a day like this.

I wonder if he'll be there tonight, because I'd love to throw down with him in the ring.

Okay, I'm feeling a little torqued over the fact he got my girl. *Girls.* Digging into that conundrum is on today's list, but first, I'm back at my office, staring at my board.

"What makes a man do this?"

Eve's voice is in my head as I look at the pictures, trying to decipher my notes. My problem is I keep all of it in my head, mostly.

Note to self—write everything down.

All of the victims are women—the youngest being seventeen, the oldest twenty-eight—most of them blonde, but a few brunette, and one redhead. A lot of them worked in the service industry, from waitresses to baristas to massage therapists and a couple dating escorts.

All were strangled, his hands on her throat, digging in. Making it personal. No fingerprints have been lifted from any of the bodies, except for Leo Fitzgerald on the body of his girlfriend, a nurse by the name of Gretchen Anderson. On her, we found not only fingerprints, but Leo's hair, maybe from when she pulled it out during their struggle.

We also found the twenty-dollar bill in her pocket.

According to my notes, we then linked Leo to all the other Jackson murders.

Lauren Delany's case, however, is unlinked. No wonder I ordered the DNA test for her.

I open the file and read through the case.

Lauren was found in September of 1997, outside a bar-slash-dive called Sonny's just off 38th Street, early in the morning by a garbage man. She'd been dead for hours, her body stiff.

She was nineteen and had been working the streets for two years. A runaway from Sioux Falls, South Dakota, she wasn't even listed in our registry. Eve somehow managed to link her prints to a prior arrest in a town just west of here, for drug possession.

Who are you, Lauren, and did Leo kill you?

I return to my desk, where sits a half-eaten roast beef sandwich from Dayton's downtown deli, one of my favorite haunts with Eve, especially when we're working late.

I wonder if we still work late together. Asher's words are still pinging in my head, *It's simple, man. You never asked her to marry you.*

Back in my original timeline, I was an arrogant, driven cop, determined to impress my chief, John Booker. I might have even wanted, someday, to take his job.

I'm not sure why I was so driven. I know it had to do with my brother, Mickey's death, and my need for justice and a kind of absolution. But more, I think I wanted Eve to fit into my life…not me into hers.

Then she got pregnant. I'd like to say that changed everything, but having a child didn't register on my life plan. It took me three months to propose.

Then Ashley came along and changed everything. My heart, my mind, my goals.

Especially since I almost lost them both during the delivery. Eve bled, had an emergency hysterectomy, and my girls became my entire world.

I was forty-five years old, and seeing how close I came to losing them, well, for the first time, I knew real fear.

I'm not sure why that didn't happen this time. All I can imagine is that I'm still my old, stupid, selfish self.

Perfect.

Clearly, I don't deserve Eve, and I've always known it. The Rembrandt in this timeline might be at the top of his game, but he's a real jerk.

I know you agree, so save it.

"Hey boss, I got some coffee."

I look up and Zeke with the man bun walks into my office like it's a practiced event. I've mentioned that he reminds me of a younger me, back when I drove my Camaro and thought I was something. He puts a cup of coffee on my desk and then steps back. "Director Burke said it'll take a day to process, but she hasn't found any DNA yet at the crime scene. She's waiting for the coroner's report before she names it a Jackson killing."

Director Burke. I let that go in one ear and push it out the other. Grabbing my coffee, I approach the board. "So, let's sum up.

What do we know about Leo Fitzgerald?" Yeah, I know you can see what I'm doing here, but for the sake of argument, let's say it's a teaching tool. A way to help Zeke step outside the box and see something new. For both of us.

"He's mid-forties, and the camera outside the parking garage," he points to victim twenty-two, "caught a shot of him in a T-shirt, with some kind of tattoo on his upper arm. A forensic artist drew out the tat, and suggested it was the work of a local artist."

I've seen the tat before. I know because it nudges a place inside me. You know how it is—when you've seen an actor, or heard a song and you know you have a memory attached to it, but you can't grasp it? Like that.

And now it's going to keep me up long into the night.

The tat is of two hands, gripping each other, wrapped in barbed wire that also encircles the upper arm. The word BRO is inked on a ribbon that winds through the art.

"Have we talked to the artist?"

Zeke looks at me, frowns. "He died, three years ago. Right before Chief Booker."

Booker. Who was killed when he tried to apprehend Leo at his house. I read the report in the last timeline, and it looks like the crime hasn't changed.

Somehow Leo Fitzgerald knew Booker was going to storm the house, so he rigged it to explode, then vanished, leaving Booker in a box.

It doesn't say, but I wonder where I was when all this was going down.

Maybe I—as in young me—needs to start keeping a journal. I also make another mental note to read up on the tattoo artist.

"Right." I smile at Zeke, like I knew that, and take a sip of coffee.

"Anything else?"

"You thought he might have served, given his bomb-making skills, and we linked his DNA to the 1st Infantry, although after he separated, honorably, from the army, he dropped off the radar."

"Right. Until he killed his girlfriend in January of 2000." I take another sip of coffee. "How did you get into police work, Zeke? You grow up around here?"

By the expression on his face as Zeke turns to me, I know I've stepped in it. "What—Boss, don't you remember the scared straight talks?" He's laughing. "It's like every time you came home from being undercover, you had a new life lesson for me. You were like a nosy uncle. I couldn't escape you."

A nosy uncle? Who is this kid? "Did you get into this because of me?"

"Of course I did." He frowns. "I thought, if the cop who put my dad in jail cared enough to make sure his son was okay, then maybe being a cop wasn't just about finding justice, but making sure lives were put back together, too."

That was *me*?

"How is your dad?" My voice is cool, but I'm making another mental note.

"Seventeen years left on his second twenty." He shakes his head. "I really can't believe he's my father. He makes me sick. Changing my last name wasn't enough. Mom still wants to call me Samuel, but you were right. Zeke is a better name, right?"

Zeke. As in Ezekiel?

Samuel Ezekiel. I'm staring at him, the memory clicking in.

Samuel Ezekiel *Swenson*, from my last case.

The one back in 1997. Oh, you know what I mean.

But… "Remind me how long your mother's been remarried?"

"I think they're going on twenty years."

29

Kincaid. "Your step-father adopted you."

"Yeah. Of course. He knew I didn't want to be Robert's son." He frowns. "You okay?"

I'm suddenly thinking of Asher's words. *Probably he's just mad because you won't let him adopt Daphne.*

I wonder how Eve feels. Does she want Burke to adopt her?

Does Daphne want to be my daughter?

I shake the question away and turn back to the board. "Why can't we find Fitzgerald?"

"He's good. Never leaves DNA on the body, never shows his face and his pattern is irregular, although he's killing with more frequency."

"Yes. As if he's getting hungrier or more desperate to be noticed."

"Or caught. I was reading an article that after a while, the game grows old. They *want* to get caught."

I shake my head. "That's a myth. Serial killers love their work. They hone it, and they become empowered the longer they get away with their crimes."

Turning away from the board, I return to my desk. "But eventually, they make a mistake. And that's what we have to look for."

A plan is forming in my mind, something sparked by what Eve said.

We have to stop him.

I glance at my watch. I put it on this morning because, well, it feels like it belongs on my wrist. A sort of tool I can use to wiggle out of this frustration that holds me hostage. But I can nearly hear Booker's voice thunder in my head.

Here are the rules. The biggest one, the one that is never, ever to be broken…Don't change the past. You don't know what else you could change, and you could totally screw something up.

Right. Check.

"I don't know why you still wear that thing. It doesn't work." Zeke says as he sits down across from me. He props his ankle up on his knee, grins at me. "What is it, a good luck charm?"

"Something like that." I rub my hand over the face, the gears showing through the transparent assembly. It's an ancient watch, with a worn leather strap and *ahem*, it does work.

Thirty-eight lost lives says it works, and that I screwed up, and badly.

I can't do it again.

"You missed our workout last night," Zeke says as he gets up. "Catch you at the gym tonight?"

I sigh, then nod, because I have to hit somebody.

He leaves. And I'm looking hard at the watch. Then at Lauren Delany's case.

When I open the file my breath catches. Eve has written a note.

DNA is a 98% probable match with Leo Fitzgerald.

Chief Inspector Rembrandt Stone, you might be a jerk, but you're brilliant.

We can stop him, Eve. I just have to find him in the past, before he kills his girlfriend. I find the file on the tattoo and look up the notes. The artist's name is Chad Grimes and he used to own a shop off Lake Street called Midtown Ink.

What if I went back and did nothing? Well, nothing except arrest Leo Fitzgerald.

There's a knock on my door, and a woman pokes her head in. "Inspector Stone, there's a man asking to talk to you. He's in interrogation one."

"What's his name?" I'm getting up.

"Arthur Fox. He's here about his daughter."

Huh? I follow her down the hallway, then into an anteroom we use for casual meetings. It overlooks the skyline of Minneapolis, and right now, the sun casts a golden shimmer against the tall IDS Center.

Arthur Fox is standing at the window.

I remember him, of course, but I'm not sure if he knows me. He's the watchmaker, the man with the answers, but as he turns, his expression suggests he has none. Only questions.

He's wrecked. In his mid-sixties, Art wears a button-down shirt, tucked in, a pair of suit pants, but his eyes are cracked and he's unshaven, as if he's stopped caring. Or maybe thinking. He's always reminded me of an older version of Mel Gibson, sort of wild-eyed and always thinking. Now, his brown eyes pin me. "Have you found her?"

I open my mouth, then close it because, as you can imagine, I'm not sure which *her* he is referring to, his wife, Sheila, or his daughter, Meggie.

I've met them both, although not together.

Sheila died in a car accident that I prevented in the last go-round. So, hopefully she's still alive.

Meggie is Art's daughter, who helped me understand time-travel theory.

His beautiful, young, twenty-something daughter…

A fist is forming in my gut.

"My wife can't sleep. She drives the streets at night, praying she spots Meggie. But…"

Oh no. I press my hands to the table, and it looks like I'm being earnest, but really, I'm just holding myself up.

Not Meggie.

"Art," I say. "I'm so sorry."

And that's when he glances at my watch. Back to me. "Is it

still working?"

I don't know why, but I put my hand over my watch as if to protect it. "Um…"

Then Art just looks at me, so much in his eyes I walk away and stand at the window. "It's not that easy. I…" I take a breath. "I have a daughter."

"So do I! And she's missing!" He steps back. "And I remember you. You came to me, years ago and…you told me that you'd traveled through time."

I don't know what to say.

"You told me that watch brought you back to your cold case."

I close my eyes.

"You changed things, didn't you?"

"Art. I—"

"My daughter was alive, wasn't she? She was alive before you changed it!"

I round and stare at him. "She was alive last time I saw her, but…" I close my mouth, but maybe he has to hear this— "But your wife wasn't. She'd been killed in a car accident, and you…you were paralyzed."

He takes a breath, closes his mouth. Swallows. "I see."

"Art, I don't know what happened to make Meggie go missing—"

"You know her."

"I do." I meet his eyes, and my throat thickens. "How long has she been missing?"

He frowns. "You worked the case. You were at my house—"

I hold up my hand. "Just, humor me. How long?"

His glare could turn me to ash. "A week now."

"And when did you last hear from her?"

He swears. "She called me from work, late, and said her car

wouldn't start, that she was getting an Uber home."

"And did she?"

"Her phone was found outside the diner where she worked."

Diner. "She's a waitress?"

He nods, and my heart falls. Oh, Art. I walk over and put my hand on his shoulder. The gesture reminds me of a place we've been before. "Art, I promise you, I will find Meggie."

His eyes are wet when they meet mine. "You could go back. You could stop him."

Him.

"Art—"

"Isn't that what it's for? To fix things?"

"No—it's not. There are rules—"

"What rules? My daughter is missing—"

"And *my* daughter is alive. And if I change something, then she won't be."

He is staring at me. "Are you sure of that?"

Pretty sure. But I say nothing.

"What if you only…what if you only stopped the murders. Changed nothing else?"

The thought trickles into my head—well, it was there already, let's be honest. But the last two times I went back to save lives. To deliberately change everything.

So, let's just revisit this idea…what if, this time, I go back and just find Leo and arrest him. And, except…well maybe I could stop Burke from getting burned, too. And Danny from dying.

But that is it. Nothing more.

But if I changed nothing then…Ashley stays gone.

And what about Daphne?

"Art. It doesn't work that way. You told me yourself that just my being there would change a thousand tiny things."

Tears are running down his cheeks and I have to look away. "My wife is married to someone else. My former partner hates me, and I have a daughter I don't talk to but…" I look at back at him. "But they're happy. I think. And what right do I have to mess that up?"

He takes a breath. "You don't have a right. But you do have a responsibility. To the one who gave you the watch."

Booker? But I'm wondering now if he doesn't mean something bigger. Fate? God? I'm not sure who is the original wearer—or maker—of the watch. But even as he says it, a ripple goes down my spine.

Listen, if you have the watch, you also have your cold cases. Solve them. Methodically. One by one. Don't skip any. And don't ever forget that you have people's lives, their futures, in your hands. Booker's words, my last journey through time, when he discovered I had the watch.

I turn to Art and put my hand on his shoulder.

"I will find your daughter, Art."

He offers a nod.

I leave out anything else.

A *responsibility.* The word hangs on me as I head back to my office, the sun low. I suddenly don't want to go to the gym.

I want to go home and sit in my daughter's room, find her stupid teddy bear, Gomer, that doesn't exist and remind myself that this isn't my real life.

But I'm right, aren't I? I don't have a right to mess up Eve and Burke's lives.

I close the door to my office, sit down and pick up my cell phone.

Because I just have to know.

Eve picks up on the second ring. "Rembrandt?"

35

I picture her sitting in her lab, her auburn hair pulled back, maybe looking through a microscope. She probably has a half-open Snickers bar next to her, a cold cup of coffee and a microwavable dinner long forgotten in the microwave.

Wow, do I miss her.

"Any update on the shoe mark on her shirt?"

"Working on it. It's a size 11 hiking boot. We think it might be military, but Silas is still trying to track it down."

"Eve, can I ask you a question?"

"Mmmhmm."

"Are you and Burke...I mean, are you happy?"

Silence. And I'm still a jerk, because who asks that—

"Yes. Of course we are." But her voice has softened, and inside it contains fragments of my memories, the good ones Eve doesn't share. I ache with the rush of them. "And more importantly, Daphne is happy."

Daphne. I close my eyes, not sure how to phrase this, but, "Should I let Burke adopt her?"

A sigh. "Rem, I think it's time you were honest with yourself. You never wanted a daughter. I mean, yes, you didn't know about her for ten years, but that's not my fault. You left, you chose to go undercover, and you never looked back. And Burke was there."

I'm listening, but my brain is hiccupping, of course. Yes, I did spend ten years undercover, but Burke and I worked *together*. After Danny and Asher died, the task force ran out of leads, and contacts and that's where Burke and I stepped in. But every time I came home, the first—very first—thing I did was find Eve. Apparently not anymore.

"You changed after my mother was shot. I don't know...you were all about not letting life be so intense, and yet, that's exactly what you did. You dove into nailing the Brotherhood for the crime, and it was like you became addicted to the lifestyle of lies and intrigue. And I get it—I've always known you were driven and passionate. But you can't have that life and this life. And now you're Chief Investigator, and we have these killings, and...Rem, you don't have time to be a dad."

My throat is closing, and I can't speak.

There's silence on the phone. "I know you resent Burke for stepping in, and that in your head there's still a chance for you to be a good dad, but...I think the best way for you to love her is to let her go."

Let her go.

"She is a lot like you, Rem. Bright, passionate, she's artistic and loves to draw. Funny."

Yes, I know this child. My child. My Ashley.

"But, the truth is, Burke is her dad."

Burke is her dad.

"Okay, Eve," I say, before my throat closes. "If this is what you want."

She's quiet again, then, "It doesn't mean you're not her father. Or that you don't love her. But, like I said, maybe love is letting her go."

I nod, but she can't see that. So I just make a noise and hang up.

See? I take off my watch and shove it into my pocket. Then I get up and head to the gym.

Because yes, I have to hit something.

Anything.

Starting with me.

Chapter 4

I am an old man. Every bone in my body aches as I stare down Zeke, my muscles burning, my skin on fire from the sweat drenching my body.

But I'm not going down. And Zeke knows it.

I told you he's like me, right? And now I know why—because apparently, I've taught him all my moves.

He has my number.

But I also have his.

"Ready to tap out, kid?"

Zeke is bleeding from where my glove met his big, trash-talking mouth.

I like him. A lot.

Around us, in Quincy's, the radio is loud, 38 Special's "Rockin' into the Night" banging off the high pipes and hard cement surfaces. It adds juice and verve to our fight, and I smack my mitts together, moving my feet to avoid his jab.

In a nearby ring, a couple of MMA boys are grappling, but I've never been into judo, bringing a guy down to the mat to wrench his body into submission. MMA is cheating. No, give me good old-fashioned fisticuffs.

Zeke is more of a slugger, like me. Which means he's willing to take a hit to land a hit. I've clearly been working on my footwork, because my muscle memory has kicked in and I'm turning into a combination fighter.

He throws out a jab, and I jerk back. He's not storming forward, mostly because he knows I can hit. He's trying to lure me forward.

It's not going to work. I stay back, play his game. I feint to a cross, then a left and again I have him guessing.

Then I feint a jab and strike with a straight right.

Zeke falls against the ropes, bounces back.

Ah, he's tough.

We've attracted a crowd. I glance around to see if Burke is in the mix, and just manage to cover up when Zeke sends a left hook.

It zings me.

He laughs, and I do too because this is exactly what I needed to work out the knot inside my chest.

I haven't a clue what I'm supposed to do. Responsibility—I lose the word in the ring, operating on pure adrenaline.

I slip a straight punch, and land a jab, then an uppercut, and bounce away.

I've winded him, and he holds up his hand, bending over. And I have the craziest flash of memory. We're in the ring, but he's young—maybe twelve, and he's wearing headgear and padding. *Use your whole body to punch. You half-commit to anything, and you'll find yourself on the mat.*

It's my voice, I recognize it, but the memory is new.

It belongs to this Rembrandt. The one whose life I've overwritten.

I'm so stunned, I drop my hands.

And you know exactly what happens. That kid sees it and lands a killer hook.

I'm on my knees, and he's standing over me. "Boss, are you okay?"

I taste blood and run my tongue against a cut inside my mouth. He crouches next to me. "Sorry—"

"Naw, Zeke. I let my guard down."

I look at him, and he holds out his glove to me.

I let him help me up, walk over, take out my mouth guard and spit out blood into a cup. Grab a towel and hike it around my neck. Turn around.

"Now we're both bleeding," he says, and grins. His teeth are red.

Yeah, I like this kid. And the feelings that stir in my chest are deeper than this twenty minutes of sparring.

I probably need to leave before I get attached. And that thought rattles me, because it's so old Rem, before-Eve-Rem.

The Rem who rarely let people in. Eve told me once that I was hard to get to know.

Only because I wasn't sure anyone would like the guy they found. Probably I was right about that. The only person I let in was Burke, although this time around maybe not even him.

Yes, this would have been me if Ashley hadn't come around when she did. Later in my life.

When I had worked out the kinks and realized I wanted something more.

Like I said, I don't deserve Eve, then or now, but I'm suddenly aware how lucky I am.

Was.

"We're done," I say and head out of the ring. Zeke is behind me and we pull off our gloves, dump them and head to the locker room.

He's out of the shower before me—probably because he moves faster— and is dressed and packing his bag. "Hey. A bunch of us are going down to the Gold Nugget. The Twins are on."

Right. My old haunt, back before my evenings were filled with playing games of Candyland and enticing my wife with a glass of wine. I wonder how Jericho Bloom, the bartender, is, and if he still knows to pour me a glass of Macallan and water when I walk in.

"Not tonight, thanks." I follow him out and notice he slips into an Audi.

My vintage Porsche, bless her, is waiting for me and purrs home to Boston's "Peace of Mind."

The house is lit when I get home, and I see Asher's little orange Kia in the driveway. I hear voices in the back as I go in and walk through the house to find Asher sitting on the deck, the grill lit. He's talking with Briana, who is wearing a pair of short-shorts and a pink T-shirt. She's pretty and cute and I hope Asher has good intentions.

Apparently, I've suddenly turned into a father.

Oh brother.

"Remy!"

The voice—I turn and Shelby is coming through the back door, holding a cool beer. She presses a kiss to my lips.

Again, I'm so shocked I don't react.

I glance at Asher, and he's grinning at me. He wears a T-shirt and a pair of jeans and is manning the smoking grill.

Is this a double date?

"Oh, Remy, you're bleeding." Shelby reaches up and I grab her wrist.

"I'm fine."

"You should get some ice on that."

Please don't call me Remy again. But I don't say that—not yet. I'm waiting.

Maybe I have a stupid name for her, like sugar bear.

This me, I do not know. I remember Shelby, sure, but how...

"Don't tell me you went down to the gym?" She touches my hair—then my chest and she's way too handsy, really. "Sparring with Zeke again?"

Huh. I nod.

"I remember when you and Burke used to spar." She lifts her beer to her lips. "Eve and I used to go to Quincy's just to watch you."

My guess is that her eye was on Burke, and now I have to ask. "Why didn't it work out between you and Burke?"

I know it's abrupt, but I'm fresh out of Minnesota nice. Shelby lifts a shoulder and for a second, I think there might be hurt that flashes through her eyes. "After the fire, he just...he just didn't want to see anyone. I mean, anyone but Eve."

Anyone but...Eve?

I frown. "What do you mean?"

"I don't know—after she lost Danny, it was her way to find peace, I guess."

That's right. Danny died in the same fire.

My mind slips back to, well, yesterday, at the hospital, where her mother was undergoing surgery. To Burke's hands on her shoulders, comforting her.

In a different timeline, the right timeline, that would be me comforting her. Me holding her when she got the terrible news about Danny and Asher. Except, she didn't get that news, because of me, ahem, and instead it's Burke who she turns to as she waits for her mother to survive.

Where was I? Clearly not wrestling Burke to the ground,

telling him to stay away from my woman.

I have a serious bone to pick with young, stupid Rem.

In this timeline, Burke and Eve healed together, and that's just not a bond easily broken.

I don't have a right to break it, having blown it the first time around.

"I thought you wanted to be a detective," I say to Shelby as Asher hands me a beer. I stare at it and shake my head. I've been down that road.

"What happened?"

She walks over to the grill, where the burgers are frying. Admittedly, it smells good, and my stomach whines.

"Seriously, Rem?" Her mouth tightens. "Let's not go there, okay? I'm over it, and you should be too. Not everyone is cut out to be a cop. To pull the trigger. I get it, believe me, I'm reminded every time I see Burke."

I haven't a clue, but deep in my gut, I know I'm somehow to blame, so I just nod. "Right. Well, you seem to be killing it at … your current job."

"Taking clients out to lunch, closing deals and looking good." She winks.

There's no heart in it.

"I'm going change clothes." I head toward the door.

Her hand is on my back. "I'll go with you."

I freeze, turn. "Shelby."

She's grinning, and oh no…no, Rembrandt Stone, what kind of fool have you been?

"You missed me. I know you did." She has her hand pressed to my chest and is backing me into the kitchen. And I haven't panicked like this since I was fifteen and invited Mitzy Owens over to my house. Mitzy was three years older than me and had things on her mind that I was just starting to understand when my father walked in.

No one is going to walk in on me.

I own my house, my life and…

And I belong to Eve.

I drop my workout bag, I take Shelby's hand, and move it off me. "Um, I…I need to do some work."

I've hurt her, and I hate that so I touch her face. "Thank you for coming over. Can we get together, maybe tomorrow night?"

And I don't know what I'm saying. But I'm a coward.

I don't want to break up with Shelby until I have my footing.

Maybe this is my life.

Maybe this is the woman I'm with.

I pull her into a hug. "You're a good person, Shelby. Just give me some time."

She holds on, and then backs up and I see something in her eyes I don't expect.

Love.

It's genuine and sweet and I'm a tool. So I kiss her, sweetly, nothing of suggestion in it, but enough for her to know that she's not being tossed away.

She gives me a smile. "See you tomorrow." She hands me the beer as she leaves.

I pour it out and drop it into the recycling bin, then pick up my bag, head to my office and turn on the light.

My cold case file box is still sitting on the floor, apparently the one constant in all my time shifts. I search for Delany's case, and after a moment, realize it's at the office.

The next one is Fadima Mahad. I pull it out and set it on my desk. Look at it.

Mother of two, shot outside her sister's house. I press my hand on it.

I can't do it.

Even if I go back, I'll do something stupid and who knows what I could come back to.

I'm about to get up to leave when the phone rings.

Eve's beautiful face lights up on my phone. I swipe to answer. "Hey."

"We got him, Rem. Leo Fitzgerald. I got his shoe print on the back of Hollie Larue's shirt—and it matches the one found in the mud at the Meggie Fox scene."

I still.

Because the name is falling through me, hitting me.

"You found…when did you find Meggie Fox?" And my voice is hollow, the air sucked out of the room.

She pauses, and I imagine her playing with the heart charm on her necklace, as she is wont to do when she's thinking. "Yesterday morning, remember? Early. Her body was found in Minnehaha Park. We worked the scene, then you went back to your office."

Minnehaha Park. Miles away from the restaurant where she worked.

"Right." I say.

Art's face fills my mind. Why didn't I contact him? Maybe because about then my brain was overwritten.

I sink back into my chair. "And you're sure it's Fitzgerald's print?"

"It's a step closer. We just have to find him." She pauses. "Hang in there, Rem. We'll get him."

She hangs up and all I can see is Meggie, leaning against the door frame of her parent's home. *Want a lemonade?* She made it tart, like her mother's.

And I killed her.

Thirty-nine.

I've killed thirty-nine women.

Not really, but you know what I mean. I lean forward, my elbows on my desk, my head in my hands as Asher walks in.

"Hey, Rem. Your watch fell out of your bag."

I look up and out of reflex, reach for the watch.

He puts it in my hand, and even as he does, I hear it.

A tick.

I look up at Asher. "You wound the watch."

He's frowning. "Yeah. Sorry. It wasn't working, so—"

Oh, it's working. And I glance down at Fadima's file. "Thanks," I say because I'm not sure exactly what happens when I, um, chronothize—*Meggie's* term, ironically.

Asher turns to leave and I hold onto my desk, hearing the locomotive rushing toward me, the sound of time reaching out to grab me, pull me back.

But it will be different this time, I swear it on my daughter's life.

Both of them.

This time, I'll stay away from Eve.

This time, I'm going back for only one reason.

To stop Leo Fitzgerald.

CHAPTER 5

I suck in a breath of frigid air and every bone in my body seizes. I'm just blinking into the world of my past, something I'm still not quite used to, and the cold is a rude concierge.

Minnesotans never really forget the cold. The way it turns your teeth brittle, smarts your nose, digs into your pores like icy blades. I'm not being dramatic—a freezing wind from the plains of Canada, sweeping into your face can turn a knife inside your cavities.

It's something we learn to live with in exchange for the glorious Minnesota summers. And at the dawn of June, the last—very last—thing on our minds is the brutal cold of winter.

I'm wearing my wool trench coat and as my surroundings focus, tighten, I realize I'm standing in the street. In front of me is an old burnt red Chevy caravan. Glass from the driver's side window splatters the cold pavement, and inside a woman is slumped over, her body still belted in.

She's been shot in the head, given the blood and tissue debris on the interior.

Fadima Mahad, age twenty-eight. She's dressed in a jilbab, her body covered from neck to toe. Her head scarf has been torn away, and I already mentioned the head shot, but I also see a knuckle bruise on the side of her face.

The first time around, the idea of someone stopping poor Fadima and her children—there are two of them, ages eight and ten—hitting her, then shooting her in the head turned a dial inside me.

I couldn't wait to get my hands on the assailant.

Now, seeing it again, my anger is ready to boil over because whoever did this will also cause the deaths of her children.

And I have kids on the brain these days.

Murmurs lift around me, and I recognize voices.

No, I recognize *Eve's* voice.

She's talking with Silas, about what shots to take, but her voice is so different from the one I just heard on the phone...

This one contains a sense of vibrancy, the hope not yet stripped out. Or maybe I'm just imagining it. Maybe I just want her, now, to still believe in us.

No. Stop, because I came with the intent of not changing anything. Not reaching back to save us. It's just that I'm like a dog to a squirrel when I see what I want.

Overhead, the sky is dour, gray, and a brutal wind lifts my collar, chafing my skin. Across the street, a dog barks behind a chain link fence. I turn back to the car and peer in.

The Standish area of Minneapolis is a quaint, well-kept neighborhood with small bungalows from the 1930s, many of them remodeled, with alleyways and sidewalks and enclosed front porches. Children walked to the nearby Bancroft Elementary school, armed with backpacks, winter coats, scarves and mittens.

They walk like Minnesotans— fighting the wind off their face, their chins tucked into the collars of their jackets, their shoulders hunched over. A couple kids glance at me as police officers scoot them around the crime scene.

I nod at them. Give them a look that says it'll be okay. That this sort of thing doesn't happen in their neighborhood, and I'll find the perpetrator.

"It's a through and through, so I'm guessing the bullet is still in the car." Eve comes up to me wearing a puffy winter jacket, a stocking cap with a pompom, and blowing on her purple, crime-scene gloved hands. Her auburn hair pokes out of the back of the white cap, her hazel green eyes just skimming over me before she looks back at the car.

She seems distant, even though we're standing inches apart.

"Drive-by shooting?" she asks. "What a tragedy."

"I don't think so. This was deliberate. She's stopped in the middle of the road, and if she was moving, she would have ended up against one of the sycamores. Or maybe the stop sign." I gesture to the sign at the end of the block.

"Instead, she's sitting here, outside this house, as if waiting for someone."

The house I'm talking about is a green and white bungalow with a small front porch and a tidy walk to the front door. I glance up and see someone standing at the window. The curtain falls.

I see you, Maryam. I'll get to her in a bit—she's Fadima's sister, and she saw the whole thing, I know it. Except, she wouldn't speak to me the first time around. Burke managed to get some scant facts from her—that Fadima worked as a classroom aide, and that she'd come to pick up her sister's kids on her way to school.

"So, it was someone she knew?" Eve asks.

"Maybe. But the bigger question is—where are the kids?" I point to the open door, to the lunch bag dropped on the floor between the seats, the abandoned backpack.

Eve draws in a breath. "They must have run."

"Or were taken by the assailant."

Eve glances up at me and gives me a drawn look. *How are you?* I want to ask, because I miss her so desperately, but maybe I saw her last night.

Oh, I hope I saw her last night.

"I'll get Burke to search the area. Maybe go over to the school. They might have run there."

As I say it, a tiny frown dimples her forehead. "Why would you ask Burke, and not Shelby?"

I'm stymied. Nothing emerges from my mouth as Eve just stares at me. The wind tosses her hair across her face and from behind her, I see a few flurries stir in the air.

Why *not* Burke? I glance around for him, and my gaze lands on a woman climbing out of an unmarked car, just pulling up to the row of cruisers. She wears her blonde hair back in a tight bun, a long black, puffy jacket, a pair of boots, a badge around her neck.

Shelby?

I think I say it aloud because Eve's mouth tightens. "Oh goody. Your partner is here."

I'm so struck by her tone that I turn back to her, but she has moved toward the caravan, looking inside. "Silas, I found her purse. Let's bag it."

Silas moves past me, glances over his shoulder. "Hey, Inspector Stone." He gives me a smile.

This is new. Silas, in our entire history, has always considered me a threat to Eve, believing in his gut that I will only hurt her.

He's probably right, so the smile is a little unnerving.

Why am I no longer a threat?

"Hey, partner." Shelby's voice—of course I recognize it because I just left her. But now she's a little bit more business, a little less come-hither and I step away from the crime scene and turn to her.

She's not wearing as much makeup, her expression solemn. "You know, if you wanted to ride together, we could. It's going to get slippery out today with your wheels."

My wheels. My beloved Camaro! I dearly hope I had it repaired after I used it to stop a drive-by shooting, well, I guess it would be four months, ago, right?

Dates are hard, especially when it feels like only yesterday. Because, you know, it was yesterday…

Not ready for time travel humor yet? Loosen up.

I look around briefly, but don't spot the Camaro. I'll find it later. Now, Shelby is telling me what she knows about the 9-1-1 call.

"The neighbor called it in. Said she heard screaming, and then a shot. By the time she got to the window, the assailant was gone."

"Did he take the kids?"

Shelby whitens. "There are kids involved?"

I gesture to the back seat, where Eve is now bagging the backpack, the lunch, and scanning the car for the bullet.

And why is Burke not my partner?

The question is on my lips, but I'm already feeling unraveled and I fear my frayed ends will show, so I just nod. "They might have been taken. Or maybe they just ran."

Shelby looks at the graying sky, her jaw tight. I agree. It's going to get cold tonight, a blizzard blowing in, and if we don't find these kids…

Well, you know the rest. Although maybe I've already changed the outcome, because clearly Burke isn't here, isn't on the case.

"Let's go talk to the 911 caller," Shelby says, and gestures toward the white and green house.

My guess is that the sister saw everything, right?

I follow Shelby to the door, pretty sure we're going to get the same cold shoulder runaround as before. Fadima and her sister are refugees from Somalia, and they're not exactly copacetic with cops.

The door opens and Maryam stands there. She is wearing her house clothes, a pair of pants and a long-sleeved shirt, but has donned a turquoise scarf to talk to us. She's pretty—dark skinned, deep amber brown eyes.

"Yes?"

Shelby introduces us, then asks, "Did you place the 911 call?"

Maryam looks out at the tragedy on the street and her eyes begin to fill. Then she nods.

"Can we speak to you?" I ask, and she draws in a breath.

"Please?" Shelby adds. "We need to piece together what happened."

"I don't know what happened." Her voice is small, her English skewed with an African accent.

But she presses a hand against her mouth and nods. "Come in."

Shelby goes in first, looks at me and says, quietly, "Let me do the talking."

Huh?

We walk into a small family room. The floor is hardwood, the furniture spare. A table on the other side of the room is filled with books and bowls filled with rice, some kind of meat. Breakfast? The place smells of seasonings—curry, coriander, and I'm brought back to the Somali World Market where I chased down Hassan, the warlord for the Brotherhood, a gang that operates in these parts. Now, Hassan is a two-bit criminal, dealing in human trafficking and drugs. Later, in my world, he'll be a much bigger problem, with real power, fingers in the police force and an empire he builds on a dry-cleaning and laundromat business.

Baby steps to an empire of crime.

Shelby asks Maryam to sit on her sofa. It's covered with a sheet. She complies and Shelby sits beside her.

I already know most of this conversation, right? She and her husband Yasir immigrated from Somalia three years ago, along with their two daughters. Fadima joined them just six months ago, with her two children, straight out of a refugee camp. Fadima works at a local school as an aide—she was a math teacher back in Somalia.

I'm partially listening, checking for anything new as I look around the room. A few books, written in Arabic, some school supplies, a backpack by the door.

On this particular day, she came by to pick up Maryam's kids for school. But before Maryam let them out the door, she heard a scream, then a shot. Looked out and saw a man running from her sister's vehicle.

"Is she…" Maryam says, and I glance over as Shelby takes her hand and nods.

"Your sister is dead," she says, and it's both straightforward and gentle. I have to give Shelby props. It took me years before I nailed that combination.

Frankly I'm not sure I ever did. Burke was the compassionate one.

But I'm working on that, right?

Maryam presses her scarf across her face and makes a keening sound.

I look away, my chest tightening.

As she cries—wailing, really—I am looking at pictures on the wall. School pictures of her two girls. I haven't asked where they are, but when I glance over at the stairs, I see two little girls sitting on the steps. They're wearing long skirts and sweaters, their hair in cornrows. I step over to them, but they get up and scamper upstairs.

I turn back and see Shelby with her arm around Maryam.

Okay, so I didn't see that coming. I also notice a picture on the table beside Shelby. I walk over and pick it up. It's a wedding photo, and I recognize Maryam, but it's Fadima, I think, who is in the bedazzled white wedding dress, head scarf and crown. It's a large group—the groom in a suit, wearing a sash, others in traditional garb of reds, golds and green dresses. Her husband wears a beard, although its close-clipped, and a black Muslim prayer cap.

"Who is this?" I ask and point to the groom.

Maryam lifts her head. "He is Talib, Fadima's husband."

"Is he here?"

"Oh no. She left him in Somalia. He is a criminal."

Huh. There's a story there, I know it, but before I can ask, the door opens.

In walks a man, mid-forties, solidly built. He wears a white long-sleeved shirt under his unzipped coat, and a stocking cap, covered slightly with snow.

So, the weather has picked up.

He looks at me, then at Maryam and Shelby and launches into what must be Somali. Maryam untangles herself from Shelby and stands up, firing back.

He takes a breath, then turns to me. "My wife is done talking to you."

This part, I remember, so I take a breath. "My name is Inspector Stone. I'm with the Minneapolis Police Department, and we're looking into the murder of your sister-in-law." I gesture to the scene outside, the coroner's van that has now pulled up. "She was shot outside your house this morning, and her children are missing."

His mouth thins to a bare line, and he swallows, glances at

Maryam. There's a little psychic conversation that happens between them, because Maryam looks down and he stares at me again. "We know nothing about this."

"She called 911," Shelby says and gets to her feet. "And she saw a man running."

"She saw no one." He steps into the room, bushing past me and heading over to his wife. Puts his arm around her. "She is traumatized and scared. You must leave."

I'll bet she is, but I don't say that.

"What's your name, sir?" Shelby asks.

"Yasir Isse. I have a green card and all my papers—"

"We don't need those," I say to Yasir. "We just need to find these children."

This moves him because he looks out to the street with a sort of panic in his eyes.

"They're missing?"

"Yes," Shelby says, and the softness is gone. "And anything you can do to help us find them...well, it's going to get cold out there."

He draws in a breath, then looks at me and shakes his head. "I don't know where they are. And neither does Maryam. Please, leave us to grieve."

Shelby looks at me, and we do our own psychic conversation.

Her: He knows something.

Me: Yes, but we're not going to get it out of him now.

"Okay, thank you for your time. And if you think of anything, give me a call." Shelby says this and hands her card to Maryam. Yasir takes it.

I step out into the brusque cold, Shelby behind me.

"It's colder in *there*," she says, and gives me a wry smile. "But, did you see his shirt?"

57

No, I didn't. Somehow, I was fixated on the way he was looking at me, a sort of hot challenge in the air.

"Laundromax Dry Cleaners," she says. "I saw it when he put his arm around his wife."

Hassan's dry cleaning company.

"Should we call Burke?" Shelby asks as we head down to the street.

Eve is standing away from the caravan, with a clipboard, probably cataloging evidence. I'm aware of her quick glance my direction, her eyes on Shelby, then away.

So we've both lost friends in this version of time.

"Why would we call Burke?" I ask as I watch the coroner pack up Fadima's body.

"Because he and Inspector Mulligan are heading up the Brotherhood gang task force?"

He and…Danny? I look at Shelby, trying to disguise my surprise, and barely bite back a *since when?*

But I know better, so I nod. "Right. And Hassan runs the Laundromax operation."

Shelby nods and reaches for her phone.

"I'll call him," I say.

Because I need to get to the bottom of this defection. I might not be able to change it, but at least I'll know why, right?

Aw, who am I kidding? Maybe it's best if I don't know. Best if I try not to care.

Because caring means changing and we're not going to screw that up this time, right?

"Let's get the patrolmen out looking for these kids. Check the park, and the school. In the meantime, we'll see what Eve has turned up. If we can figure out who shot her, maybe we can figure out who took the kids."

I'm looking for Eve—don't worry, I'm all about the case—but she's vanished.

And, I'm also scanning the cars for my Camaro.

She's not in the lineup on the street.

But I do notice a sleek black Corvette, with a removable top, now dusted with snow. What are the odds?

"Are you sure you don't want to catch a ride with me back to the crime lab?" Shelby says. "Your Corvette is going to skate on these roads."

You know I'm fist pumping inside even as I glance at Shelby. "Naw, I'll be okay. I'll meet you there."

"You got it, Remy."

What—?

I kind of scowl at her and she's grinning. "Just trying it out for size."

"No."

She lifts a shoulder. "Stay on the road, partner."

I know I said I wouldn't change things, but really, *Remy?* C'mon, you'd do the same thing, admit it.

It's not like I've torn a massive hole in the cosmic time-continuum.

Yet.

CHAPTER 6

One look at the sky told Eve she was running out of daylight. Even at noon, the pallor over Minneapolis appeared deathly gray, with white stuff peeling from the sky and blowing across her third-story lab window in her downtown office.

Three stories below, the plows were out, cars slowing as the slush accumulated.

They were running out of daylight, with two kids missing. And the forecast was laying down the first real blizzard of the season.

She'd lost her appetite the moment she spotted the backpacks in the car. And it hadn't come back as she pulled the evidence and sorted through the young mother's belongings.

Her purse doubled as a getaway bag, everything from toiletries—three toothbrushes, paste, shampoo, a comb and brush—to protein bars and energy drinks. A wadded ball of socks, a scarf and lip gloss. And inside the zipper pocket a wad of twenties.

"It's supposed to get down to the single-digits tonight," Silas said from his work table where he was preparing the bullet they'd found lodged in the passenger side door for a ballistics test.

"Hopefully we'll find a match with one of the weapons already in the system." She was opening one of the inside zipper pockets of the purse.

"My guess is that it's from a 9mm. The ammo is 94 Grain Steel Case," Silas said.

"Could be a Ruger LCP. It's the most popular handgun used on the streets."

"If we find a match with a bullet already used in a shooting, it might lead us to the gun, and then back to the shooter."

"Mmmhmm." Eve didn't add it, but she was hoping it was a shooter that Inspector Stone—Rembrandt—could track down and question. And maybe, if they were all good enough at their jobs, and a little lucky, they might find two lost children before the cold could take them.

"Hey," Eve said. "I found a picture of the kids."

"Make a copy of it and send it to Stone. He can distribute it."

She took it over to the scanner, and sent it through to her computer. She could attach it to an intra-department text.

Then she'd bagged it and labeled the image of two children probably ages eight and ten with their mother in a photo booth. The image settled into her brain.

She'd nearly lost her own mother four months ago, and she was an adult. She couldn't imagine the terror of seeing your mother shot before your eyes. At least when her mother was shot, during a drive-by shooting, Andrew Burke had been protecting her with his body.

Rembrandt had been racing to protect her father.

Both men were heroes in her book.

Burke, maybe, felt guilty, however, that he hadn't protected her mother because he'd shown up at the hospital later. Stayed with her during her mother's surgery while Rembrandt booked a suspect they'd been chasing.

Sometimes Burke still came around after his shift, just to buy her a drink.

At least someone still noticed her.

Oh, she was just being petty. Rembrandt was just training Shelby—and frankly, she was happy for her friend.

Just not happy that Shelby had started to refer to Rembrandt as Remy. As if they were buddies.

Or something more.

Stop. She went back to the purse and tugged out the wallet. Opened it.

Rembrandt wasn't the kind of guy to step over the line of partners.

Okay, maybe he'd stepped over the line a little, with her. But Shelby was his direct partner. And he, her mentor.

Sure, she and Rembrandt had gone on a couple dates after he'd apprehended her mother's shooters.

Still, something seemed off about him, one minute all in, the next, focused on something—or someone—else.

Maybe he just wasn't into her. And shoot, Shelby wasn't helping. Her friend seemed to have turned her attention off Burke and onto Rembrandt and frankly, the way she looked at Rembrandt, just irked Eve down her to her cells.

And Rembrandt had certainly set Eve on the shelf when Shelby walked into his life. Or maybe he just saw her as Danny's daughter, and that made things complicated.

She should have moved away after graduating from the police academy, to pursue her passion for crime scene investigation far away from the Danny Mulligan reputation. Her father's shadow leeched into everything she did.

Eve wanted her own reputation, one built on her own abilities, her own detective work. Not the one that identified her as Danny Mulligan's daughter.

"You've been staring at that wallet for a while now. Anything interesting? Or are you still thinking about Inspector Stone and *Shelby…*" Silas said.

"I'm thinking about those kids who are lost," she snapped. "And the fact that Fadima Mahad has a pass to the St. Mary's Haven of Hope women's shelter in her wallet." She pulled out the paper pass, with Fadima's picture on it. "Clearly she felt like she was in trouble."

"What kind of trouble?"

She set the pass on the scanner and ran it through, added it to her files. "I don't know. But I'll pass it along to Rem—Inspector Stone."

"Oh, don't tell me we're back to that." Silas walked over, the bullet in a plastic bag.

"Back to what?"

"You are driving me crazy. I thought you two went out."

"Twice actually. But I don't know. Ever since Burke asked to work with my dad, and Shelby joined R—Stone, it's just—"

"You're jealous!"

"I'm not. I'm…" She shook her head. "I'm nothing. I'm not letting the man get under my skin. Focus. We have kids to find."

Silas looked at her. Sighed. "He can't commit, Eve. I've told you that. He might be a charmer, but deep down, if you want to find someone who will stick around, you need to look somewhere else." He took the label that had printed and pressed it on the bag. "Like Andrew Burke."

"We're just friends."

"He likes you."

"He used to like Shelby."

"And you used to like Rembrandt Stone. Everybody's happy."

"Get away from me."

Silas grinned. "I'm going down to the testing range. I'll be back...have fun..."

It was the tone of his voice that made her turn. Aw...

Rembrandt Stone was swaggering—okay, her word, maybe not exactly—into her lab. But shoot, he looked even better than he had this morning, the snow melting into his dark hair, turning it a little curly at the ends.

She remembered winding her fingers—stop.

He'd scraped it back, away from his face, and wore the slightest hint of a beard, as if he'd rolled out of bed early.

Or never went to bed? No, no...

She should probably go stand outside in the cold for a minute or thirty.

"Hey, Inspector..."

"Inspectors," Shelby said coming in behind him. "Hi, Eve."

Oh brother. But she noticed the tiny crease in Rembrandt's brow.

"Hey," he said, as he walked over, his voice low. "What have you found out about Fadima?"

She walked over to the items she'd pulled out of Fadima's purse, now spread on a table. "Her address on her driver's license is the same as her sister's so I'm not sure where she really lives. She's twenty-eight, and is a donor."

She pointed to a couple drawings. "I think these might have been made by her children. A boy, his name looks to be Ahmed—" She pointed to the scrawled name on the paper, the D backwards. "And the girl is Hadassah."

A lined page with a flower in pencil. Hadassah was written in English on the bottom.

"We have patrols checking the local school now," Rembrandt said, and she looked up at him. It was weird how he could nearly read her mind.

When he wanted to.

"Good," she said, all business. "I found these in the backpack." She walked over and picked up a pair of mittens and a hat. "These belong to Hadassah."

Rembrandt grabbed a purple glove and used it to pick up the backpack. Fluorescent blue and covered in stickers of horses. "Get any prints off these?"

"Nothing in the system."

"Where's Ahmed's pack?" Shelby asked.

"Maybe he's still wearing it, maybe not."

"Did he drop his lunch?" Rembrandt pointed to the paper bag.

"Nope. Take a look." She pointed to a nearby plastic bag.

He smiled then, a hint of amusement in his eyes. "Are those… Happy Meal toys?"

"Yep. From the Disney movie, *Hercules*. Me thinks someone was sneaking his toys to school." But even as she said it, she saw a miniature version of Asher, scared, alone and with his *Hercules* action figure to make him brave.

Her smile vanished around a thump of her heart.

"We'll find them," Rembrandt said quietly, again reading her brain.

Or maybe it really wasn't that hard to figure out what they were all thinking.

"I have an idea," she said, turning to her workstation. "I found this in her purse."

She handed him the day pass in the plastic baggie. "It's for a women's shelter in downtown."

He took it, looked it over then handed it to Shelby.

"Why would she stay there, if she had a place to stay at her sister's?" Rembrandt asked.

"Maybe it wasn't safe anymore at her sister's house," Shelby said. "Maybe something happened that made Maryam not want her around anymore."

She looked at Eve.

Eve met her gaze. "Or maybe Fadima trusted her sister, and then suddenly, her sister started kicking her out of her life."

Rembrandt looked at her, then Shelby. "Um, Shelby, can you go get me a Snickers bar?" He pulled out a dollar from his pocket.

Shelby looked at him, frowned, then, "Sure."

Eve folded her arms, looked out the window.

"I know it's none of my business, but...are you okay?" he asked as Shelby left. "Are you and Shelby having a fight?"

"Nope." She looked back at him. "Everything is fine."

And then he laughed. *Laughed.* She rounded on him but he held up his hand. "Just, breathe. It's just...c'mon Eve. It's me. I know you, and that tone of voice. Everything is *not* fine."

What? She cocked her head. "What do you mean, you *know* me? We went out on two—count them—two dates, and then suddenly, nothing. A couple hot kisses, two dates and you're out? No calls...you're a ghost in my life."

He seemed to recoil at that, his expression turning to something like confusion, or maybe panic. "I'm not...I didn't..." He blew out a breath, as if yes, that's exactly what happened.

So. The truth was she didn't mean near as much to him as she'd thought. He just didn't know how to break her heart.

"Don't be jealous of Shelby."

"Don't be stupid."

"Eve." It was the way he said it, low and soft and—.

Sheesh. Get over him already.

"Eve, look at me." He said it quietly, as if he *did* know her.

She didn't know what it was about Rembrandt Stone, but she never had a bone to resist him. Gritting her jaw, she looked up at him. Took a breath.

His blue eyes held hers, something painfully raw in them. "I'm sorry for whatever I did to hurt you. Sometimes I'm…I can be a real jerk. I know it." He lifted his hands, as if to touch her, but dropped them again, put his hands in his pockets. "I promise you, working with Shelby is just as surprising to me as it is to you. But it's my job to train her, so I need to do my best, okay?"

She lifted a shoulder.

"Eve—"

"It's fine. It's not like we were dating or anything."

"We weren't?" And he bore so much—maybe *hurt?*—in his voice she couldn't help but stare at him.

"Did you think we were—"

"I…well," He ran a hand behind his neck. "Yeah. I thought we had something real. But I get it." He formed a smile. It didn't meet his eyes. "I guess we all have to move on, don't we?"

Oh.

Yes.

Apparently.

"Here's your candy bar, Rem." Shelby came back into the room.

Rem.

That's what Eve called him. Or *had* called him.

"Thank you, Inspector Ruthers," he said and took the bar from her.

Then Rembrandt turned to Eve and handed her the Snicker's bar.

For her?

She took it, but he held it for a second. She met his eyes.

"Everything is going to work out, Eve, I promise." She didn't know why, but the words shimmied down, into her bones.

He was probably talking about the missing children, but it felt…

No. Hadn't he just said it was time to move on?

He turned to Shelby. "We're going to check out that women's shelter."

"Sounds good."

"I'll meet you there."

The fact they weren't driving together in his hot new Corvette did almost as much for her mood as the Snickers.

Shelby stood there for a moment, and Eve reached over and grabbed a copy of the pass from the printer. "Find those kids." She offered a smile.

Shelby nodded, smiled back.

"Call as soon as you get that ballistics report back," Rembrandt said.

"I will, Inspector."

"Rem," he said, and winked. "C'mon, Eve, we're still friends, right?"

She hadn't a clue what they were.

All she knew is that she probably needed to open a window.

CHAPTER 7

Keeping my new wheels on the road as snow starts to thicken is a little tricky. Corvettes are made for summer driving, for speed and sitting down in the curves, with wide sports tires.

Tires that become skates on a little snow and ice.

Thankfully the plows are out and dusting the road and right now the accumulation melts nearly as soon as it hits the pavement. But I have my wipers on and snow is dinging against my glass top. Overhead the sky is dismal, the wind fierce as it picks up debris along sidewalks and tosses it into the gutter.

Did I mention that the Corvette is a convertible, T-top, with deep-sitting leather seats and a nice throaty V-8 engine? I'd like to turn on some Eagles and take it easy down some lonely stretch of highway, the wind in my hair.

But now, I'm in stop-and-go traffic through downtown. I apply the brakes and slide to a stop at Portland and 19th, just under the 35W bridge. Overhead, the traffic is at a near standstill, drivers hesitant in the growing storm.

I know I'm not supposed to care, but did you think Eve was a little chilly back there? What's with the inspector business? We're past that.

Problem is, I get around Eve, and the old Rem starts to spiral out, the one that knows that she belongs with me, and…

Okay, I promise, I'll do better. No more Snickers bars.

No more, *c'mon, Eve, we're still friends, right?*

But what's a guy to do when clearly, *so clearly*, the chump I was hurt her.

I really hope young me isn't interested in Shelby, and the fact that I can't stick around to have a little chat with the schmuck…

I'll leave him a note. Tell him that Eve…what? Ends up with his best friend?

As soon as I find these kids, find Leo Fitzgerald and leave, the better for all of us.

At least, I'm trying to tell myself that.

St. Mary's is a battered women's shelter, and of course I've been here before, twenty-three years ago. I know what will happen—we'll arrive and ask to see Fadima's room, and the director, a kind but strict nun named Ana, will tell us to get a warrant.

Which we will. But we're busy looking for the kids, too, see, and thirty-six hours later, when we have our warrant, Fadima's room will have been cleaned and reassigned.

So, my mind isn't really on the shelter, and what we might find, but on the sky, and the fact that in less than forty-eight hours, two children are going to burn to death.

I forgot to call Burke, so there's that too. But frankly, yes, I'm a coward.

I don't want to know why he, um, *left* me.

Let's not talk about how that sounds. I turn up my radio, and John Mellencamp has no mercy with "Hurts So Good."

I turn him off and pull up behind Shelby's cruiser. She's probably right to drive this beast, especially today. I might have to walk home.

The shelter is located in a historic Romanesque Revival home donated to the city, probably by a Pillsbury. The wide walkway leads up to the stately home, made of sandstone bricks, with a terrace, an arched entrance porch and two turrets. It looks like it might have been an apartment building once, but now the place has 90s high-tech security, with a camera mounted on the porch and an intercom system at the door.

The wind is tossing snow onto the steps and I shiver as Shelby presses the doorbell. A voice answers and she gives our names and asks to speak to the director.

I turn and watch traffic as we wait. The place sits across the street from an icy, barren parking lot, a Family Dollar store, a car rental by-the-hour shop, and just down the road, a church.

The door opens. It's funny how I don't recall these people until suddenly, they walk back into my memory, as if they've been standing in the shadows. Ana is exactly how I left her of course. She wears a skirt, a sweater, a wooden cross on a lanyard, and nun's habit.

Sister Ana. She's thin-boned, a little lined in the face, but bears the presence of an MP as she stands sentry at the door. Her eyes narrow. "Yes?"

"We're investigating the murder of Fadima Mahad. She was a homicide victim outside her sister's house today, and we know she was staying here." Shelby gets right to business, and I'm a little impressed.

Sister Ana is shaken, just for a moment, her hand going to her cross. "I see," she says, and it occurs to me that maybe she's familiar with these situations.

Wonder if she feels as helpless.

You have a responsibility, Art says in my head, and maybe I do.

Shelby shows Sister Ana the picture of the pass. "We really need to get in and see her room."

Sister Ana, predictably, folds her arms over her chest. "I'm sorry but—"

And this is where we get turned away.

"Her two children are missing."

Nope, tried that last time, too.

Silence, and I look at the Sister, back to Shelby, who wears a grim look. "Please, Sister. I understand your rules for privacy, but we think she might have been murdered by a man—someone who knew her—and we need to find those children." Shelby looks at the sky, then back to Sister Ana.

The sister's mouth draws into a line.

"I can get a warrant," I say, and Shelby gives me a look. What? It's true.

"Okay," Sister Ana says.

I'm gobsmacked.

"Just you," she says to Shelby. "You, wait here."

Me? Sure.

I'll just hang out here on the porch, no problem.

Shelby disappears inside.

This is new. But if it saves the kids, I'll set up camp.

I stomp my feet to keep the blood flowing. Watch a sedan pull into the dollar store parking lot.

Maybe I should call Burke and tell him our suspicions.

I put up my collar. The wind has started to whip the snow sideways, the lights blurring across the street.

Yes, I'm irked that he left me. I'm a good partner. And sure, we had our fights, but we had each other's backs.

Or at least I thought so. And now I'm playing out that future conversation in my head. *Why did you leave me?* It sounds a little like something out of *Fatal Attraction*.

So what that he left me. It's not like I wasn't prepped with this knowledge—after all, you remember what Asher said. Burke and I haven't been friends for a long time.

Still, the whole thing puts a fist in my gut.

I'm blowing on my ungloved hands—way to go, young Rem, let's not dress for the weather—when Shelby comes out. She's thanking Saint Ana, and I manage a smile, too.

Then the door closes, and Shelby holds up something in a plastic bag. She's also wearing purple gloves, the little overachiever.

"What is that?"

"It's a note left in Fadima's room. She was indeed living there, with her two kids, for the past two weeks."

"So Maryam lied to us."

"Looks like it. She had a change of clothes for herself, and her kids, and a tidy little room there."

"No sign of the kids?"

"I think Sister Ana was being straight with me. The kids aren't here."

Well, it is a bit of a hike from here to the crime scene, maybe four miles.

"What does the note say?" I'm getting really cold, and I wouldn't mind if we had this conversation over a cup of coffee.

Except, I can't justify a cup of coffee when all I can think about is Fadima's children.

I need to check the house.

What house, you ask? The house where the children—and Burke—will burn tomorrow night. You gotta keep up.

"I don't know," Shelby says. "It's written in Arabic."

"What?"

She gives the bag to me.

"Got any more gloves?"

Out of her pocket she produces a fresh pair. I wonder if she has an entire bag of them in there.

Shelby is a regular Girl Scout. I'm starting to feel bad about turning her down for the job all those years ago.

I open the plastic bag and take out the note.

"Do you read Arabic?" she asks.

I'm dying to say *yes, I'm fluent, aren't you?* But I'm trying not to be a jerk, so, "No. But my guess is that Eve could find someone."

Shelby nods, and I see the tiniest flicker of hesitation, maybe even hurt in her eyes. Enough of this.

"Shelby, what's going on with you two?" I put the note back into the plastic before the snow smudges it.

"Nothing."

"I'm better at my job than that." And I am, but I also know women—or at least *my* woman, and she's already clued me in, so, "Is Eve ticked at you for making inspector?"

Shelby frowns. "What? No. It's not that…"

And I'm flashing back to my previous timeline, which is probably, in part, this timeline, and, well, I possess the unfair advantage of knowing what *will* happen, so… "Did something happen between you and Eve…and Burke?"

Her breath catches, and she makes a face, wrinkles her nose. "What? No, it's just…you know. After the shooting, he was just… around her a lot."

He was? How *a lot*? But I've learned that sometimes it's best just to keep quiet, let a woman's thoughts spool out.

"We had something, and then, I don't know, he started paying more attention to Eve, and I think he likes her."

"I'm sure they're just friends." But I'm a liar, because I'm *not* sure of that. But I'm not getting involved, remember?

But I push a little, for my own good, and get, "She's ticked off because she thinks you and I have something going."

She looks away.

Aha. I knew it. Still, "Why does she think that?"

Shelby lifts a shoulder. "I might have said something."

I'm staring hard at her, trying to see inside her head to anything stupid I might have done to encourage her.

"I'm sorry, Rembrandt. I know you and she dated. And I know she liked you, too."

I'm so relieved by her omission of any guilt on my part that I pin my lips together to keep it from escaping. "It's no problem, Shelby. But just for the record, we only work together, okay? Nothing more."

"Yes, of course."

Now I'm in a soap opera. "Listen, how about you bring that paper by the lab, and then go back to the neighborhood and help the patrols search for the kids."

"Where are you going?"

I head off the porch. "I'm following a hunch."

It's her laughter that stops me.

I turn. "What?"

"Burke. He said to watch out for those."

"Hunches?"

She goes to her car. "He said that one too many hunches of yours could get me in trouble." She's still laughing.

I'm not.

Because I suddenly know why Burke left me.

Have I mentioned how I hate time travel? It's like handing chocolate kisses to a kid and telling him just to look at them.

I know stuff. I care. I change things. And I can't seem to stop myself.

Getting in the Corvette, I turn the radio up to curtail any dark thoughts. Styx screams out "Renegade" as I crawl over to the Powderhorn Park neighborhood.

I know you're thinking—Rem, they won't be there yet! But it's worth a shot, and what would you do if you knew two kids were out in the cold?

I take Portland down to Lake, going easy between the lights, and finally turn left on Lake, down to South 17th Ave.

This location, I remember. And yes, it helps that I looked it up, but wouldn't you remember the sight of seeing two children screaming from an upstairs window? Feel the heat of the flames shattering the lower story windows, blowing through the door?

Taste your panic as your best friend ran into said inferno? Yes, I'll admit it, Burke is-slash-was my best friend, and there was no way I was going to let him die.

We fought for real, right outside in the grime and slush and I didn't let him win.

But I paid for it. Burke was never really the same after that. More serious, driven. He'd disappear into his music on the weekends, and some weeknights, and never married.

I wonder if he feared having his own children and the nightmares that might return.

So, of course I spot the house easily. It still looks like it could blow over in a stiff wind. The house is three stories, with a wide porch. Pale yellowed paint peels off the siding, and plastic from a window whips against a broken pane.

The third story window, from a jutting dormer, is completely gone, and the snow is accumulating on the sill.

I stop my Corvette outside, and frankly, it's like a beacon blaring, *Please, rob me.* I lock the car, pocket my keys and head up the broken concrete steps.

The door is locked, but one hard turn of the knob breaks it free and I head inside.

The smell could drive out the dead. Cat urine, burned plastic, and maybe even rotten eggs. I put a hand over my mouth as I walk inside. Blankets piled in corners, refuse in the front room and a stained mattress litter the floor—I do notice original oak planks, something Eve would appreciate, but I push that out of my head.

Wallpaper peels from around windows and off the wall in great strips. It looks to be imprinted with faded roses, and I wonder if this house was, once upon a time, loved.

All it needed was a little commitment, someone who cared.

The ceiling is falling, stuffing peeking out of the lathe and plaster walls. Paper litters the floor, and as I walk, the boards squeak.

I walk gently. I don't want to go through to the basement and be trapped for all time. A stairwell in the middle of the house runs up between the main room and the dining room. The kitchen is in the back. The refrigerator is gone, but an old stove sits without burners, or an oven door. Someone built a fire in the cavity and probably nearly burned the house down because soot darkens the wall behind it.

The sink is black with filth.

I can't imagine how, or why, Fadima's children found this place.

I take the stairs up to the second floor. Two bedrooms and a bathroom. The bedrooms contain filthy mattresses, more blankets and I see a few needles, some condoms.

I find the final stairs and they lead to a tiny attic space with the dormer window.

It's dark, and the small space smells of rat and bat droppings. In the dim light of day, and through the grimy windows, I search the room.

No cold children.

So maybe they're not here yet.

And the bigger question is…will Burke ever be here? Of course I want to save the children, but…what if I've already changed time?

Burke didn't work with Danny, before, of course. So, what if his new assignment means he doesn't find these children, doesn't get burned, doesn't…end up with Eve?

I'm not here for that. Really.

But I don't hate the thought as I head downstairs. On the second floor, I find another set of stairs—it looks like they lead down to a porch in the back.

A thump sounds, then footsteps at the front entrance. I freeze, and it's one of those times I'm glad I carry a weapon.

Okay, yes, I should calm down. After all, it might be a couple of kids.

Or it could be just a homeless man, seeking shelter.

But it could also be any number of drugged up runaways who have clearly used the mattresses on the second floor as a temporary flop house.

I creep down the back stairs and slip into the kitchen.

More whining of front room boards.

It could be the kids, so I'm not leaving. Instead, I move toward the door. A loose board under my foot betrays me. *Shoot,* I can do better than this. I might be young and able—and we haven't even talked about the fact that this body is ripped, fierce, and one I miss dearly—but I'm a little rusty on the sneak and peek part of my job.

I reserve that for when I put Ashley to bed on Christmas Eve and have to check if she's awake before Santa shows up.

And there I go, thinking about Ash, and how, right now, I should probably say screw it to fate and hightail back to Eve's office and tell her I'm still painfully crazy in love with her, and it's going to get worse with age and—

Another squeak and a breath catches. I hold mine and flatten myself to the wall.

"No one needs to get hurt here," says a voice.

My heart slams against my chest. I *know* that voice.

But really, Rem, who did you think you'd find? Leo Fitzgerald, the serial killer?

Hey. Don't mock me—fate is like that.

"Just throw any weapon you have down and come out with your hands where I can see them."

I turn, and step out "Burke—"

It's not Burke.

In a second, I'm on the floor, my face in the grime and dirt, a knee in my back, my hand in a submission hold.

And Danny Mulligan is in my face, upside down as he looks at me.

"Stone?"

It's a second of silent disbelief.

The boards break beneath us and suddenly, Danny and I are falling.

CHAPTER 8

Between the two of us Burke has always been the calm one.

When we first met, he was fresh out of the military. You've already met me, so you know how I am. Burke? He's the straight shooter, a solid guy, and one who thinks before he acts.

We're a good team. I can count on him to have my back. Which is why it doesn't surprise me that as I start to fall, Burke is the one who reaches down and grabs both of us, saving us from crashing through the floor into the dungeon of this house.

Burke has a hold of my collar and we haven't punched through far, just a couple boards broken to let us through the joist. The smell that billows up from the lower level could be a biotoxin.

Something died down there. And I might not be kidding.

We backpaddle fast, coughing. I get up, a hand over my nose. I'm trying not to breathe the putrid smells as I stare at Burke.

Then Danny.

"Why did you tackle me? I had my hands up!"

"Sorry." Danny is breathing a little hard.

Danny's dress pants betray the filth of tackling me. He's wearing a leather jacket, his ID on a lanyard around his neck. Every time I see him it's a little like seeing a ghost because as you know, I didn't know Danny well before he died in my original timeline, and then I saved his life and now he's here. Alive.

Tackling me.

I'm not sure if I'm going to save his life again, but for now I don't want to get on his bad side. Danny Mulligan is a decorated cop, a legend on the force, and he's Eve's father. Even if Eve and I don't end up together, I secretly always wanted Danny to like me.

I'm not sure why. In my first timeline, my father and I did not have a particularly close relationship, so maybe it stems from that. The one thing I've always admired about Danny even though I didn't know him well was his focus. Danny brings an intensity to his investigations that feels a little like a bull running through the streets of Pamplona.

I don't know what they're working on, but the same intensity sparks in his eyes as he looks at me. "I thought you were someone else."

"What, a homeless guy? Sheesh."

"No," Danny says. "One of Hassan Abdilhali's gang members."

Oh, so he's still on that case. I guess I could expect that since two of Hassan's guys tried to kill him in a drive-by shooting. Of course, this was after he killed Hassan's brother in a shootout that saved my life. So maybe Hassan was really after me. All I do know is that Eve's mother was nearly killed in the crossfire. I can see why that might make this guy a little bit driven.

"You okay?" Burke asks.

I am. Although I feel the need to change clothes. I nod and brush off. Burke turns to Danny. "I told you that was his Corvette out there." He looks over at me and grins.

The smile is so unexpected I just stare at him, wordless.

84

Because, you know, he's angry at me. Now, or, maybe then, in the future. You know what I mean.

"What are you doing here?" Danny mutters. He's also dusting himself off and twisting his nose from the foul odor coming from the basement.

Maybe, and probably, the sewer backed up.

"Let's get out of here." I move towards the door and they follow. "I was looking for a couple of kids—you know, that homicide over in the Standish neighborhood this morning?"

"I heard about that," Danny says. "It's all over the radio."

"The kids are still missing, and it's getting colder out." I make it outside and breathe in the frigid yet clear air. The snow is already a couple inches thick. Heavy snow. Slick and dangerous.

I probably need to take the Corvette out to the farm and park it for the winter. When it's white out, I drive a 1985 4-wheel drive Jeep. I'll have to wait till tomorrow when the streets are clear and then head out to Waconia. I can also check on my parents and see how they're faring in this new version of life. I might have mentioned it, but my brother Mickey disappeared when I was twelve, he was eight. The police found his body just recently in a lake near our home.

You can imagine what kind of bite that took out of our family—sixteen years of not knowing where your son is, whether he's dead or alive.

Last time I visited them, they seemed to be better than I'd ever seen them, but, of course in my timeline my mother had a stroke when that news was delivered. So I suppose anything is better than watching your mother deteriorate at age fifty-two.

And it hits me, now, that my mother is the same age I am.

I suppress a dark shudder as Burke comes out and stands beside me. "You think the kids were here? Why?"

I look at him. "I don't know. Just a *hunch*." I can't help myself. There's a little piece of me that's still needled that Burke would request a transfer because of my *hunches*.

I mean, so what a guy has a gut feeling? Most of my gut feelings worked out. Like how about saving eight people from getting burned alive? Or saving Danny and Asher's lives from a drive-by shooter?

You and I both know they weren't just hunches, but *Burke* doesn't know that. I think he's being a little—

He looks at me and laughs. One deep chuckle that rumbles under his sternum.

I don't know what to make of that.

Danny walks out. "We need to keep looking."

"Who are you searching for?"

"We arrested one of Hassan's gang members and he said Hassan was making meth in one of these abandoned houses in the Powderhorn area, so we're doing some random checks, going from house to house."

"Meth?"

"Yes. It's homegrown—Hassan's trying to find a way to fight the business of a new threat in town, a Russian gang headed by a guy named Alexander Malakov."

I've never heard of him, but Burke's words remind me... "By the way, that woman who was shot today is the sister of a man named Yasir Isse. He was wearing a Laundromax shirt when he came home today. My gut says that he's working for Hassan."

"You think Hassan is behind these missing kids?" Burke asks.

"I don't know. The investigation is still ongoing. But, it's cold out..."

"Yeah," Danny says. "You can't ignore any leads." He's standing with one foot on the step. "By the way, how is she working out?"

Of course, I'm thinking he's talking about Eve because who else would be referring to? But that's such a weird question to ask me, especially since I know he doesn't want me to date his daughter. So. "Who?"

"Shelby," Danny says, with a tiny frown. "I approved her application and was going to have her work with me until Burke asked to be transferred to the task force."

I don't show any surprise because I probably already know this information but really? That's how she got in—through *Danny?*

I wonder if her relationship with Eve has anything to do with that.

"She's doing fine."

Danny nods. "I think she'll be a good investigator. She just needs training." He pulls out his phone. Glances up at me as he answers it. "She reminds me a little of you."

Then he gives me a smile.

It has the effect of an atom bomb, bursting through my bones to my cells. It's a rare genuine smile, a smile of acceptance, a little humor, and maybe even respect.

A smile I've never seen before.

I just stare at him not knowing what to do with that.

He turns away, answering his phone, and heads out to his car.

Burke turns to me. "Nice of you to train Shelby."

Did I have a choice?

But he's about to follow Danny, and it's now or never. I take a breath, because I *have* to ask. "Burke, why did you ask to transfer to Danny's task force?"

He lifts a shoulder but doesn't meet my eyes. "It seemed like a good opportunity."

A good opportunity? I don't respond and Burke gives me a

quick glance. I must wear a look of incredulity on my face, because he adds, "I thought maybe you didn't trust me anymore."

He's staring out at the storm. Ice is hitting my face, but my chest is hot.

"You didn't include me when you went on that stake-out with Danny and it sort of sat in my craw and I started to wonder if maybe you wanted a different partner."

And because I'm not the guy I used to be, but one who knows his future losses, I say, "Not true, Burke. Not for a second. You're the only partner I've ever trusted."

Admittedly, the old Rem, the struggling novelist with a chip on his shoulder, would have never bared open his chest. But I've learned that time—or fate—is fickle. And you only get moments, blinks of opportunity to change your world. To say the things that matter. So, "You're my best friend, Burke. You always have been and I'm sorry that I left you out of my investigation."

He's swallowing, looking down, as if he understands we're at a precipice.

I look at Danny who's sitting in the car, the engine running.

"I'm sorry if I screwed things up between us," I finally say.

Burke just stands there, his hands in his jacket pockets. He might be a former MP, the calm one, but he's also got a heart as big as a mountain.

I realize now how I took that for granted.

Maybe he is better for Eve, and I'm shaken by this thought.

He takes a long, deep breath, as if soaking in the words. Then, still looking at the street, "Me too. I gotta go."

Right. Yep.

"But, hey." He looks over me. "I got a gig tomorrow night. Seven, at the Nebraska. Bring Eve."

I look over at him, now. "I thought you two were...um…"

"What?" He gives me a look.

"You two have been…well, I know you've been there for her…and I haven't."

"Dude, seriously? She's crazy over you."

I blink at that, not sure—"

"You can't see that? You gone blind?"

I have no words.

"You still like her, right?"

What am I going to say? She's my very breath. But maybe I'm not hers. Not anymore. Still, I'm not going to lie to the guy.

"She'll always be my girl," I say. "No matter what happens."

That's true, because of Daphne, right? But I realize it doesn't quite come out how I meant it because he looks over at me, frowns. "So…what does that mean? *No matter what happens.* Are you dumping her?"

"No, it's just…" and I can't believe these are the words that emerge, but what if Burke is her future, and not me?

What if she is better off with him? Happier?

"If she needs to move on then…" I breathe through the fist in my chest. "If she needs to move on to somebody else then I'm not going to stand in the way."

I don't meet his eyes.

"Rem," Burke says, a little disgust in his voice. "I'm not after Eve. What are you thinking?"

You know I'm thinking *exactly* that. Because he might not know it now, but he *is* after Eve. And he's going to win.

"No," I say, "but—"

"Dude! Make up your mind. Do you want her or not? Because you have the power to screw this up, or not. Don't give up so easily."

Oh bro, the game is long over.

But I wonder, too, if he's talking about us. Me and Burke. Because it's one thing to say you trust somebody, but completely another to show it.

My mind goes back to the fight we had in this very front yard. The brawl. And mostly out of pain and frustration, and the fact that two children were dying, but also the bone deep fear I had that he might die on me, too.

It cemented us. Made us who we were. Burke and Stone.

But we're not there yet, apparently.

And if I just saved his life, we'll never get there.

My heart feels like it just cracked a little bit.

"You'd better go," I say, nodding at the car.

He's quiet. "See you tomorrow night." He's down to the walk when he turns. "I really hope you don't blow it with Eve. Because I don't think she'll ever get over losing you."

I just stare at him as he walks away.

Oh, she'll get over me, buddy. Because I'm apparently going to break her heart, over and over until she's had enough.

And if I don't, then she'll never have Daphne.

Wow, this is fun, because it occurs to me that in order to leave Eve's future intact, I still have to be a jerk to her. Get her pregnant, and *not* ask her to marry me.

Young Rem, how I long to strangle you.

This *can't* be the answer.

And then it hits me.

Maybe my plan to step aside isn't for her, but for *me*. To make me feel just a sliver better about the way I hurt her in the past. And not the way *I* hurt her, but you know, *the other me*.

We were happy, once upon two lifetimes ago. Really happy. And the other me screwed that up. I don't deserve her, and I know it.

So maybe it's not selfish to want that back. Because it's *not* just about me.

What if I can do better this time around? Have Daphne, who is really Ashley, and not be the guy who screws this up.

Let's be honest—Burke was never her future until I blew it.

As he looks at me, I realize…Eve and I *do* still have a chance. And maybe, here, today, right now, I'll try and be the guy she deserves.

"Find those kids!" I shout into the wind.

He gets in the car, and I'm left on the front porch, alone, as the world turns white around me, layering the street, the grass, the trees with grace.

I'm scraping off my car when my phone rings. I pull it out, and of course it's Eve, the woman has eerie ESP. "Hey," I say as I answer, get in and turn my heater on high. My hands are frozen, and I wiggle my free one in front of the blower.

"I got a guy translating that Arabic for you." Her voice echoes, as if she's in a parking garage.

"Thanks—"

"Ballistics came back on that weapon. We don't have the gun, but the gun was used in a shooting at a gas station in the Phillips neighborhood two weeks ago. We think it might be a brotherhood killing."

The Brotherhood, the Somali gang run by Hassan Abdilhali. "Any witnesses?"

"A camera picked it up, but the tape is grainy. So far, no leads."

"Thanks, Eve. Call me when you get that translation."

We're both silent. Maybe she's not ready to hang up either.

I'm still sitting at the curb, not sure what to do. I could drive home—probably I *should* drive home. But—

"Actually, I'm going home," Eve finally says. "The roads are getting bad, and I need to shovel before it gets heavy."

Eve hates to shovel. Threw her back out once, was in bed for a week. The thought of her wrestling with the snow… "I'll meet you there," I say, and hang up.

Because we are running out of second chances, and this time, I'm going to get it right.

Chapter 9

I'll meet you there.

Maybe Eve hadn't heard him correctly as she'd hung up her phone. After all, the echo of cars exiting the parking garage cut out most of their conversation.

Still, Rembrandt's words clung to the back of her brain as Eve negotiated traffic in her Ford Escort, inching through downtown, then over on Highway 100 to 7, and finally weaving through her quaint neighborhood to her cute fixer upper in Saint Louis Park.

She pulled up to the curb and simply sat under the feathering of snow as she watched Rembrandt Stone, dressed in jeans, his wool coat, no mittens or a hat, and a pair of flimsy dress shoes, shovel her driveway.

He'd already finished her front walk, up to her broad porch, and had cut out at least half of the driveway, pushing the snow to the sides to create tall banks.

Everyone was right—Rembrandt Stone was an enigma and she was tired of trying to figure him out.

And frankly, seeing him stop, blow on his hands, then resume the shoveling just formed a burr in her chest. *What was he doing here?*

He couldn't just show up in her life, out of nowhere, and act like they'd been dating for years, like he could be the guy she depended on.

She had pulled up behind his Corvette, got out and marched down the sidewalk.

His back was to her, but maybe she radiated a sort of heat because he turned, leaning on his shovel. "Hey!"

"Don't you hey me. What are you doing here?" Okay, she didn't mean it quite like that—or maybe she did. Shoot—now she didn't know her own brain. Just that… "You're wearing dress shoes, for Pete's sake. And where are your gloves? And…I can shovel my own stupid driveway."

"I know." He leaned over and continued pushing another wide swath of snow to the side. "But it's getting heavy and if we don't move it now, it'll be frozen and impossible to clear later."

"That's not an answer. What are you doing here?" And shoot, but the snow had turned his hair all glistening and curly, and the sight of him seemed so terribly domestic that…

Well, it seeded all her crazy thoughts about what he might be like as a husband. Or father.

Stop it! What was she thinking? She didn't even want kids.

Maybe.

Someday.

But she had miles of career between now and a family. And who knew where Rembrandt would be by then.

"I'll be right back." She headed into her house, and only then did it occur to her that he'd somehow broken into her garage to get her shovel.

She opened the coat closet, rummaged through it and emerged with a hat and a pair of stretchy gloves.

It was better than nothing. When she came back outside, he was nearly done. Still, she marched up to him. "Here." She handed him the gloves and he took them.

"Thanks."

His hands looked cracked and reddened and were probably numb. She shoved the hat on his head. "Didn't your mother teach you anything?"

He opened his mouth, as if to retort, then closed it and smiled at her. "Thanks, Eve."

She narrowed her eyes at him. "Rembrandt Stone, you drive me crazy."

He grinned at her.

Oh... "Give me that." She grabbed the shovel and began to push the snow.

Okay, it was heavier than it looked. Still, she didn't need Stone showing up to...what?

Show her that he cared?

At the end of the drive, she turned, and he stood there, hands in pockets, watching her.

"I don't get it," she said, hunkering down for the next swatch of snow. "You ignore me for weeks, and now, you're shoveling my driveway?"

He stepped out of her way. "Can't a guy be nice?"

"You flirt with me, show up on my doorstep, kiss me and then—I don't know what to think."

She tossed the snow into the bank. Felt a pull deep in her back and grunted.

"Gimme that," Rembrandt said and reached for the shovel.

"Not on your life, pal," she said.

"Don't be so stubborn—"

"Don't be so confusing." She looked at him, then, fine, shoved the handle toward him.

He just stared at her, a little confusion on his face.

Oh, please. "Listen. You can't keep doing this to me. Because…yes, okay, I'm jealous. I like you. And I know I shouldn't be jealous of Shelby, but I am, okay? And just when I think I'm over you, you show up and buy me a candy bar. Or shovel my driveway and—you have to stop this."

She took the shovel back. "I think you should go."

He closed his mouth into a thin line. Sighed. "Fine. Yeah. You're probably right."

He headed down the sidewalk toward his Corvette.

What?

Seriously?

"You're leaving?"

He turned, hands still in his pockets. "Tell me what you want, Eve."

She took a long, cool breath, exhaled. Watched it form in the air, the words caught in her chest.

"I don't know what I want."

He said nothing for a long time. Then he nodded, something short and brutal and got in his car.

No.

Don't go.

She stood there, not able to move, however, because—how was she supposed to love a man she didn't understand?

Maybe this was for the best.

He started his car and eased out into the road. She set the shovel down, blinking against the bite in her eyes as she dug into the snow.

The spin of the wheels, the gunning of the engine made her glance up. The Corvette had settled into the slant of the curb and the wheels spun against the snow cover.

She hid a smile.

He looked at her through the windshield.

She looked away.

Heard the door close.

"Stuck?" she said, throwing the snow into the bank. Ugh. Her back clenched again. She gritted her teeth.

"In a manner of speaking," he said and came back over to her.

"Please let me finish this." He held out his hand for the shovel. His blue eyes caught hers, something of sincere earnestness.

And really, what was she going to do? "Fine."

She relinquished the shovel, then walked over to the steps and sat on them, watching as he finished the last two rows, quietly, relentlessly clearing a path to her house.

The sky was quiet, thick with the padding of snow, but the wind was kicking up, blowing through the trees.

He cleared the final row up to her house, then stopped in front of her. Gave her a small smile. "I'm not trying to be a hero. I just wanted to be a good guy for a change."

For a change? She frowned, but then stood up and grabbed the shovel. "Come in. I'll make you some hot cocoa."

But he stayed behind for a moment, as she headed to the door. "Are you sure?"

She turned. "What are you going to do? Skate home?" She looked at the Corvette, back to him. "Besides, you need to tell me how you got this shovel."

"Your key. Under the rock near your garage."

Right.

He smiled then, and his words returned to her, *C'mon Eve. It's me. I know you...*

What was it about this man that made her believe him? "Come

in, Rem. Please."

Maybe it was time to figure him out.

Then she headed inside.

Rembrandt followed her. She took off her jacket, hung it in her closet, then reached for his. He handed her the hat and gloves.

"Maybe I should make a fire," he said. "The house is chilly. Do you have wood?"

"In the back. Sams brought over a couple bundles."

He had taken off his shoes, now walked through her front room to the fireplace. Opening the screen, he reached for a brush and dustpan and swept the ashes into it, then dumped it into the debris bucket.

Apparently, today he was a handyman.

She went into the kitchen and put on water to boil. What was going on?

He opened the back door and set the bucket on the porch, then grabbed a bundle of wood and brought it back inside.

"Your feet have to be cold," she said, noticing wet footprints tracked across her wood floor to the family room.

"I'm fine," he said as he crouched in front of the fireplace.

She watched him a moment, and couldn't displace the eerie idea he'd done this before. Or maybe it was simply a memory, buried deep, of her father coming home during a storm to make a fire. The careful stacking of the wood, the tiny kindling sticks, the paper shoved into the cracks to get it to light. A science to it, really. At some point, he stopped and rolled up the sleeves of his dress shirt past his elbows to reveal strong, sinewed forearms.

Outside, the sky had darkened, the wind continuing to pick up, tossing snow against the pane.

He was stuck here. The thought came to her as she went upstairs to change into sweatpants and a sweatshirt, warm socks.

Rembrandt Stone was in her house, probably for the night. Trapped.

And he wasn't getting away until she dug into what made this man tick.

By the time she came downstairs, the fire was lit, crackling in her hearth.

"I've only used the fireplace once," she said as she returned to the kitchen where the kettle whistled. "Right after I purchased the house, my father built a fire to check it out."

"I love fires," Rem said, as he leaned against her doorjamb. He'd folded his arms over his chest. "When I was a kid, my father used to build one every Sunday afternoon, and me and Mickey would lay on the floor in front of it reading the Sunday funnies."

She could see him, dark hair askew, pouring over the comics, maybe playing the word games. "You never talk about him," she said as she pulled down a couple mugs from the cupboard.

"Who?"

"Mickey. Your brother." She didn't look at him but saw him draw in his breath. "You told me about how he went missing, but…but that's all." She opened a packet of hot cocoa mix and poured it into a mug.

He was silent for a moment, then, "His name was Michelangelo. After—"

"The Italian artist." She poured the water into the mug.

"My mother was an art history major. You can guess who her favorites were."

She laughed and handed him the mug. "Clever."

"Not when you're a kid. Mickey had it easy." He smiled at her over the cup. "This is good."

"We could order a pizza, but my guess is that delivery might take a while."

"Got any potatoes? I could make soup."

Really? Now the man was going to cook for her?

"I think so." She opened her fridge and pulled out a bag of potatoes.

"Meat?"

"Does bacon count?"

"Always. Milk?"

"Whole."

"Garlic, onions, chicken broth, and flour."

"Who are you, Emeril Lagasse?"

He laughed. "No. This is a Gordon Ramsay recipe."

"Who?"

"Right." He shook his head wryly, as if listening to a joke only he knew the punch line to. He grabbed a dish towel and wrapped it around his waist. "Watch and learn."

And how. She pulled up a stool to her center island. "I don't really know how to cook."

"Yet." He glanced at her and grinned, then turned back to rummaging through her drawers. She was about to direct him when he found a potato peeler. He dumped the potatoes into the sink then began to peel them. "When I was a kid, I loved snowstorms. We lived on a farm, and the next day, we'd have a snow day—" He looked at her. "A snow day in the city is nothing like a snow day in the country. In the country you have snow forts to build and drifts to climb, and a snowmobile to race through the fields."

He peeled the potatoes backwards, pulling the peel off as he drew the peeler toward him. Strong hands and she had a hard time keeping her mind on his words, watching his hands work.

"We had an old snowmobile that my father let us drive, and we'd get on that thing and go for miles. We'd go to an empty field near our house and spend hours chewing it up. I was about ten, maybe, and took out the sled after a big storm. Huge drifts on the roads, and thick between the trees, creamy white on the fields."

He rinsed off the potatoes, then found her cutting board under the sink, as if he knew it was there all along, and began to dice them.

"It was late, and it was getting dark out, and we started to head for home, hit a ditch. It was all covered over with snow, and I didn't see it coming. Mickey flew off and broke his wrist. And, the sled was stuck. It was about a mile back to the house, and I could have walked, but Mickey was only seven, so…"

He had found a pan, set it on the stove.

She slid off the stool and retrieved the bacon and the onion from the fridge and handed it to him.

He diced the bacon and put it in to fry and started on the onions.

"I was scared to death. I knew I couldn't leave him there. So, it was either freeze to death together or leave him there and hope that he'd be okay while I ran to get help."

She stared at him. He was blinking, hard, trying not to let the onion juice get to him.

"He was just this little kid, and I knew I was responsible for him. I was just sitting on the sled, crying, trying to get it out of the ditch when he climbed on behind me and said, "It's okay, Remy. I'm not scared. I know you'll keep me safe."

He wiped his eye with his wrist. "I hate onions."

She said nothing, unable to move at the sight of Rembrandt Stone crying.

"I couldn't leave him. We left the light on and it got very dark, and very cold. We sort of huddled on the sled. Mickey was pointing out the stars he knew, and I was trying to hold onto him so he wouldn't shiver. I thought for sure it was over until I saw a light breaking through the night across the field."

He dumped the onions in the pan with the bacon.

"It was my father, coming out on his sled to look for us."

He found a pot and filled it with water, then set it on the stove to boil.

"You and Mickey were close."

He lifted a shoulder.

"They never found the guy who took him."

He swallowed.

"But you don't blame him as much as you blame yourself."

"He was alone because of me."

Oh, Rem.

He looked over at her, then. "I just wish I'd been with him."

Then you might have been taken, too. But she didn't say that.

But the idea of something happening to him…

She drew in her breath.

No, she wasn't jealous of Shelby. Okay, maybe a little, but mostly she was afraid.

Afraid that she'd fall for this man, and…

She looked away, her own eyes burning.

"Hey, hey—what's going on?"

He'd set down his knife for a wooden spoon he'd pulled from a crock pot and now came over to her. "Sorry. Are you thinking about the missing kids?"

Uh no. And now she just felt worse. She blew out a breath. "I was thinking about my mom, getting shot."

"Gosh, Eve. I'm so sorry—"

"And how she was when my Dad was shot."

He went quiet. "That's when she told you all not to become cops."

"Yeah. But she was so strong. I don't think…I could ever be

that strong if someone I loved died." She looked at Rembrandt.

He nodded, and there went his enigmatic expression.

Smoke billowed off the pan. She made a noise and he turned, bit back a word as he turned down the heat. "Burned the bacon."

"I'm sure it's okay."

Just as she said it, he picked it up to throw down the drain.

"Rem!" She slid off the stool. "Stop."

He looked at her, something tortured on his face. "Rem. Just because it's not perfect doesn't mean it's not good." She looked at the pan. "Oh, c'mon. It's barely burned. It'll be fine."

He set it on the stove. "Right."

She touched his back. "You okay?"

He sighed. "I don't know. I just…" He closed his eyes. "I just want…I guess I want to believe I can make everything okay. That I can fix this." He turned to her, an intensity to his gaze that stilled her. "That you'll be happy, no matter how it turns out."

She gave him a smile. "I am sure I'll like your soup, Rem."

He was staring at her, her eyes, her face, her mouth.

And with everything inside her, she wanted him to kiss her. Because she'd been on the receiving end of Rembrandt's ardor, and right here, right now, with the storm cocooning them, and with the very real possibility that he could—would be spending the night.

Yes.

She touched his chest. Took a step toward him. "I've never had a man cook for me before."

He swallowed, and something that looked very akin to panic flashed through his blue eyes. "I'm usually a good cook…"

"Mmmhmm." She put her other hand on his chest and lifted her face to his. "I'm sorry about your brother, Rem. But you're not alone anymore."

Then she kissed him.

And he just…froze.

No response, well except for the thunder of his heart under her hand.

What—?

She leaned back. He swallowed, his eyes still in hers. "Eve, I…"

She released her hands. Took a step back, her face heating. Oh…

"Eve—"

"I'm sorry. I thought…" She turned away. "I thought—"

"You thought *right*." He grabbed her arm, not hard, but enough to turn her. And the terrible expression on his face startled her. "Eve, there is nothing more—nothing—that I'd like to do right now than…kiss you. No, I don't just want to kiss you. I want to take you upstairs and crawl into your warm bed and stay there all night and chase from your mind any thought but that you and I…that we belong together. But…" His jaw clenched and he took a breath. "But I'm trying to do things right this time. I'm trying to…" He put his hand on her face, and it was warm now, and slightly trembling. "I don't want to hurt you, and I fear that if I let myself do what's in my head, that's exactly what is going to happen."

Nothing he said made any sense.

"So, please help a guy out here, and let's just make soup. And we'll sit by your fire and maybe we grab a blanket and have a camp out, but please, don't look at me with that expression of yes, or…" He winced and looked away.

"This was not what I intended when I came over to shovel." He looked back at her. "You have to know that. I just…I just wanted to be a good guy."

And that was it, wasn't it? The mystery of Rembrandt Stone.

He was all the things she knew of him—driven to save lives, dedicated to justice and loyal to his friends, but at the core, Rembrandt Stone wanted to be the good guy. The one who did things right.

However, in his eyes, he would always be the guy who'd left his brother.

Not quite the villain, but not the hero either.

Somehow Rembrandt was still stuck out in the field, looking for the light.

"Rem." She pulled his hand away, and held it. Gave him a soft smile. "You're safe with me."

He let out a long breath. "Thank you."

"Now, make me some soup."

CHAPTER 10

The problem with my job is simply that justice is a not a healer of wounds. It doesn't bring back the deceased. It simply puts a finite end to the festering.

Healing, however, has to come from someplace else. Forgiveness, maybe, or acceptance. Or perhaps it's simply a realization that the suffering isn't wasted. That there is something precious that can be born from pain.

There's a saying on a picture in my office, back in, well, my real life. It's a quote from a speaker and it reads, *Life doesn't have to be perfect to be happy. Sometimes you have to find the happy moments between the pain.*

Maybe I'm expecting too much from life to give me a happy ending.

Maybe now is enough.

Maybe the suffering of the past two lifetimes has given me this moment inside the storm.

I'm laying on the floor, Eve with her head on my arm, the firelight flickering in shadows against the ceiling. She's playing with the heart charm on her necklace, running it back and forth over the chain, thinking. We ate our soup over candlelight, the electricity going out about two hours ago. Now, we're on our second bundle of firewood, the night soft around us.

The house is starting to chill, but we're under a blanket, and have pulled the sofa cushions onto the floor to make a sort of camp bed.

And I'm happy. And yes, I know this isn't real—not exactly, but just give me this moment.

I know what you're thinking. Rem, dude, you could be upstairs with Eve right now, rekindling the relationship you nearly let die. But you saw the earlier versions of me.

If I want Eve to be happy, then maybe it starts with caring about her, being the guy I want to be with her. And I know that sounds like something we learn in kindergarten—treat others with respect, and it's not like Eve wasn't saying yes, but what if I do walk out of her life tomorrow?

Maybe the only way I don't completely screw anything up in the future is to…well, listen to my regrets today.

And hope Young Rem is somewhere deep inside, paying attention.

Her voice pulls me out of my mental wanderings.

"Is there a case you haven't solved yet?"

She's already told me her favorite snowed-in story, one about watching horror movies in her parents' basement, and I told her a few unpublished stories about the police academy, and early days with Burke.

"Of course." Although, now that I think about it, the only current one, because, you know, the watch, is Lauren Delaney. "We found the body of a hooker near Sonny's a few months ago—"

"I remember that case. She had a footprint on her shirt."

She did? I rise. "I don't remember that."

108

She looks at me. "Huh. I thought I told you. But, that was about the time Shelby came on board, so maybe you were busy." She smiles.

I don't. Because I wasn't busy the first time around.

No, the first time around I was still trying to find Danny and Asher's killer. And frankly, Eve's mind wasn't on the game either.

She might have missed it. Or maybe Silas found it. Whatever the case—

"What did it look like?"

"A hiking boot of some sort. We were thinking it might be military."

I draw in a breath. "Yeah, that plays out right."

She leans up on one elbow. "What do you mean?"

"Our prime suspect is former military, a guy named Leo Fitzgerald." I can't really tell her how I know it's him—after all, Gretchen's death won't occur for three years. But now that the DNA found on Lauren is connected to Leo, I can add, "He has a unique tattoo—two hands clasped, tied with barbed wire, the words BRO written underneath. We think it was done by an artist from Midtown Ink named Chad Grimes. We're hoping he can lead us to Leo, or at least his last known address."

I look at her. "Oh, by the way, remember to pull DNA from Lauren's body. She was sexually assaulted—see if they did a rape kit, and if there might be DNA from that."

"Good idea," she says. "Sorry—I thought the M.E. would have done that."

It'll take a few more years for DNA testing to become standard practice, so I say nothing. "I'll find him," I say.

She murmurs something beside me and I'm keenly aware of her body against mine, of the warmth of her, and it feels so familiar, so normal, if I close my eyes, I can believe we're back in our bed, in

109

our remodeled Craftsman on Drew Avenue, Ashley across the hall. Together. Safe. The thought makes me ache to my bones.

"What evidence do they have on your brother's murderer?" Eve asks after a bit.

The fire is crackling, and it's warm beneath the blanket, despite the heat being off. I'm tired—really tired, the kind of exhaustion that comes from being awake too long, the kind of buzzing that tells you if you close your eyes, you might not open them again.

They say children fear sleep because it feels like a kind of death. Now, as Eve puts her hand on my chest, the simplicity of the gesture radiating through me, it's this tiny moment I don't want to lose.

I refuse to close my eyes.

"We have his bike, of course, and they found his shoe on the side of the road. It was muddy, so they had tire tracks, also, and they determined it was a conversion van, so they ran license plates from the area, and got a small list, but none of them panned out. I remembered a white van driving by us before I realized he wasn't behind me, so that matched with my memory, but…" Believe me, I've wracked my brain for anything—a memory of a person driving, perhaps, but even under hypnosis, I saw nothing.

It's haunted me.

"Who was assigned to your case?"

"John Booker, actually. He was on the Waconia Police Force, and it was one of his first cases as an investigator."

"Really?" She raises her head. "So you've known Chief Booker—"

"My entire life. He used to check on our family, sometimes, just to keep us informed. He was a big reason I became a detective."

A realization washes over me. That's probably why he gave me the watch.

Because I understand the way injustice digs into the soul of victims. It's almost worse than the original wound itself, festering.

"I used to have this recurring dream, where I was on the ice in the middle of a lake, and it would start to crack around me. And I'd keep running, but I'd slip and fall. And then I'd get up and start running again, trying to stay ahead of the cracking, but I never made it. I just kept running."

And that sounds so raw, I sort of need to say something, so, "I know. It's creepy."

"Someday you're going to reach the shore, Rem." Eve lifts herself up and braces herself on her elbow. Stares at me. "And I'm going to help you get there."

Then she smiles.

I love this woman so much I can't breathe.

Maybe it's the look on my face, but she touches my cheek. "I'll stop you," she says softly.

Heaven help me. I know what she means and no, I'm not that far gone, but I do smile, roll over, catch her in my arms, and kiss her.

She is soft and welcoming and puts her arms around me and makes a sound I know, and I sigh as I deepen my kiss.

Because this moment is enough. She doesn't have to stop me but it's still a challenge to finally roll away, stare at the ceiling and remind myself of who I want to be, to this Eve, my Eve.

She is beside me and it's not long before I hear her deep breathing.

And then I let myself sleep.

I wake to a ringing, something buzzing on the coffee table, now pushed against the wall. The dawn is bright through the window. Eve is still asleep, the fire in the hearth is out, although still winking with bright red embers.

The buzzing continues and I ease away from Eve, roll over and scramble to my feet. When I reach the noise, it's not my phone, but Eve's.

She's awake after my abrupt departure, her auburn hair kinky and wild around her face. "That's my ringtone," she says, and I hand her the Nokia.

She answers it, rolling onto her back. The house is still without electricity, so I get up and hike out the back.

The snow against the door nearly keeps me from opening it, but I wedge it free and grab the wood, sheltered under a tarp on the porch. By the time I bring it in to start up the fire, Eve is up, the phone tucked against her shoulder, writing down information.

I wad up the paper, add the kindling, then place the logs on top. The fire starts easily with the help of the bed of still hot coals.

The house bears a layer of chill and I pick up the blanket and walk over to Eve, slinging it over her back. I look over her shoulder at what she's writing.

Still.

"Is that—"

"Shh," but she looks at me and nods.

The translation of Yasir's note.

Fadima. Talib is in America. He is looking for you. I can no longer guarantee your safety. Don't tell Maryam where you are going. May the peace, mercy, and blessings of Allah be upon you. Yasir.

Eve is thanking someone, but I'm already headed for the door, grabbing my coat.

"Who is Talib?" Eve says, joining me. She is reaching for her coat, too, and I look at her.

"You can't actually think that you're driving your Corvette. Look at the roads."

I am. They're whitened, the snowplows woefully behind

schedule. My Corvette is under a thick layer of white, never to be seen again.

But the world is a wonderland of grace, fluffy, diamond-brilliant snow frosting the trees, the sidewalks, the roofs. And it's bright.

"Where are we going?" Eve has pulled on snow boots and I look woefully underdressed in my suit pants and dress shoes.

Plus, we're not getting out of her driveway, so it's a good thing she didn't pull in. At least a plow had come through during the night—probably she can ease her way from the curb.

"I need wheels," I say.

"No doubt."

"No, I need…" I turn to her. "Can you drive me out to my parent's house in Waconia? I need to pick up my Jeep."

She rolls her eyes. "Of course he drives yet another cool car."

"It's old. I got it in college."

"Whatever." She closes her door behind her. "So now I get to meet the parents?"

I must give her a wide-eyed look of terror because she laughs.

I love her laugh. It ignites my entire body in song.

"Calm down. I promise not to tell them we spent the night together."

Oh, I'm in big trouble with this one.

She still thinks it's funny thirty minutes later as we slow, coming into town off Highway 5. My parents live south of town on an eighty-acre hobby farm with a big white barn my father uses to tinker on his vast array of Volkswagens, Audis, and currently, my 1988 Porsche. The farmhouse is ancient but upkept well by my father. Two stories painted yellow with black shutters and a wide porch.

My father has clearly been up since before dawn because the

entire drive and yard is plowed, the front steps cleared and smoke billows out of the fireplace.

Eve pulls in the driveway. "I can stay in the car."

"You'd better come in," I say. "Or they'll hound me about you. You think I'm a good interrogator—you haven't met my mother." I give a quick wink.

My mother used to be a broken woman, overweight, confined to a wheelchair, her mouth at a sag, her eyes empty.

Now—and I still can't get used to this—I find her in the kitchen, making breakfast, wearing an orange apron, a pair of jeans and a Christmas sweater.

"Rembrandt!" She is pretty, her blonde hair cut short in a bob, and it's my resounding evidence for why closure is a worthy pursuit. Everything changed—this time for good—when my brother's body was discovered.

We still wait for justice, but it's out there, like Eve said.

Someday we'll find the shore.

"Hey, Mom," I say and give her a kiss, and it's such a normal gesture for our newly Cleaverized family that it feels like it's always been this way. She smiles, though, and pats my cheek and I see the surprise in her eyes.

I guess we've all changed, more than a little.

"I came to get the Jeep."

"I thought you'd show up." A voice from the stairs and my father comes down. He's lean, muscled, even in his late fifties, a straight shooter and take no prisoners kind of guy, and in this time, he still has his hair. He grins, grabs my hand, and clamps me on the shoulder. Then turns to Eve, not before his eyebrows give me a quick twitch. "And who is this?"

"Eve Mulligan. She's one of my CSIs."

That didn't come out right at all, and I glance at her in apology, but she doesn't seem to care and shakes my father's hand. "Nice to meet you."

"You too." Dad nods, offers a smile.

"Would you like some coffee?" my mother asks and in a second, she'll have Eve sitting at the table eating pancakes and homemade peach jam.

"Here for the Jeep?"

"Yeah."

"You might need some help getting her out of the barn," my father says and heads to the door. "We haven't fired her up since this summer."

I probably don't need help, but then again, I'm still wearing my dress clothes, so maybe.

We hike out to the car and into the barn, past my beautiful Porsche, under a tarp, and a new Audi Dad has up on jacks. I spot my Jeep.

She's a 1985 black, hard-top Jeep CJ-7, 4-wheel drive, 5 speed stick on the floor, with real doors.

My first real love.

And no, she's not a Volkswagen, but Dad forgave me for that after a while. You can't pick what you love, right?

He opens the hood, pulls out the oil stick and checks the oil. "Needs a quart."

He has one on hand and props the bottle over the oil intake while he checks the tires.

"So, are you two dating?"

I open the door, step on the brakes. They seem to be working. "Yep."

"She's pretty."

"Yep."

"She know about Mickey?"

It's funny, I think, that he would ask that. But it is the one defining moment in my life.

If she doesn't know about Mickey, then she doesn't know me, maybe. "Yep."

He retrieves the oil jug and closes the hood. "Fire her up."

I do, and the Jeep rumbles rough at first, then settles into a purr.

He grabs a rag and wipes his hands, then comes over and leans against the door. "Last time you were here, you were tracking down the murderer of a young girl. Did you get him?"

I smile at that. Good memory, Dad. But the fact I haven't updated him on that case tells me I haven't seen them in four months. "Yes. Sorry I haven't been out here—"

"Can't live on sorrys." He thumps my knee. "But we're glad to see you when you can."

And now I feel worse. "Dad, can I ask you a question?"

"Will I need coffee first?"

I turn off the Jeep and climb out. "Do you ever revisit that day, and wish you'd done things differently?"

He knows what I'm talking about, of course. We're not so healed that the wound is out of reach.

"Nope."

"Really?" I look at him.

He scowls. "Wishes and what-ifs don't change things. The only thing that matters is right now. What you choose is who you are, and the future you're writing. Get that right and you don't have to worry about the what-ifs."

I stare at him. "You don't have regrets?"

"I didn't say that. But I do know I wouldn't have done anything different. I did what I did at the time because I thought it was best. Given the same circumstance, I would have made the same choice." He clamps his hand on my shoulder. "And so would you."

I hope not. "Why didn't you ever yell at me? Blame me for—"

"For some devil that showed up on a dirt road and murdered your brother, and tried to steal your soul? Nope."

Wow. When he puts it like that—

"Son, that wasn't your fault, regardless of the way you want to rewrite the what-ifs in your head. I'm just so grateful he didn't take you, too." He offers a small grim smile.

Not me. "I was the oldest. I should have stayed with him—"

"Enough.

"But we could have had a normal life. A happy life."

"There is no normal life—no happy life—that is without pain, Rem. In fact, what if pain is part of a happy life?"

"What? Dad—"

"No, seriously, Rembrandt. Suffering makes us into stronger, better people."

"Not this kind of suffering! Dad—your lives were destroyed."

"And yet we lived through it." His other hand finds my shoulder. "And we still have you."

But, Mom had a stroke.

"Rembrandt, your life isn't written in the past. Yes, your past makes you who you are, but when you get here, you have the choice of who you want to be. Your life is written in the right now. Your choices are the only thing you can control. You have to let go of the rest. And occasionally, ask for help."

I know that. I *do.*

Mostly.

But if it means that this time, I win. That this time I get the girl, and the serial killer, and while I'm at it, save a couple of lost kids...

Then I'll take all the help I can get.

CHAPTER 11

Before we leave the farmhouse, my mother loads up a baggie with fresh muffins and it's blindingly clear Eve is their new favorite.

Last time around, I didn't introduce them to Eve until after we'd eloped, so this is new. I know what you're thinking, but I did mention that things were rough between my parents and me during our original go-round.

I'm trying to do better this circle through time.

Shelby is in my thoughts as we drive in on the snowy, salty roads. I need to call her and update her on the translation of Yasir's note.

I still have a hard time wrapping my brain around the idea that Shelby Ruthers is my partner.

I have a clear memory of her pushing me up against the wall and kissing me.

Almost like she can read my mind, my cell phone rings just outside the city, her name flashing on my screen.

"Where are you?" she asks without preamble. "I'm at your house. I thought you'd need a ride."

Right. "I went out to Waconia to pick up my Jeep. But I got

the translation of Yasir's note."

I don't mention where I spent the night, but I'm guessing she'll figure it out.

Choices. My father's words hang in my head. *Your choices are the only thing you can control.*

I don't know what fate will do with my choices of last night, but at least I can live with myself.

"What does it say?" Shelby asks.

"That Talib, Fadima's husband, is in the United States, and my guess is that means Minnesota. And that she's not safe at their house. If Fadima followed his instructions, then it's true that Maryam didn't know where her sister was staying."

"Now what?"

"I'm going to Maryam's house to have another chat with her."

"I'll meet you there. She's not going to talk to you, Rembrandt."

Right. "Okay."

I follow Eve all the way until we get to Uptown, then she heads toward the city.

I take Longfellow down to the Standish neighborhood.

The banks are piled high with snow, the plows out in force. It's probably a snow day, the kids gloriously thrilled about staying home. A few bundled children are building tunnels in the berms along the sidewalks. The snow lays heavy on the trees, a few limbs are down, and wind whisks the top layer of snow off the drifts and tosses it against the sun in tiny. chilly sparkles.

There is no evidence of yesterday's tragedy as I pull up to Maryam's white and green bungalow with the front porch. No car in the drive either, so probably Yasir isn't here. I wait for Shelby in the car, and listen to the Steve Miller Band urge me to take the money and run. Maybe. I like how this timeline is going, and I'm feeling grace in my bones.

Like maybe this time, I'm doing something right.

But not if these two kids are already frozen.

Shelby's car pulls up behind mine and she gets out, wearing her down jacket, her badge around her neck. I feel like a bum in yesterday's clothes.

"Hey," she says. The air captures her breath. "Still nothing on the kids."

"I'm thinking that Talib found Fadima and took them," I say.

"Is it horrible that I hope that's true?" She's looking at the kids in the yard, bundled up and playing in the snow. "That although Talib is a killer, I hope that he's kept the kids warm and safe last night."

"Not horrible at all." We head toward the house—the drive-way is plowed, the front walk shoveled—and Shelby rings the doorbell. Nothing, so she hits it again.

Finally, the inner door opens and it's not Maryam but a little girl who answers. She looks about ten and is wearing her hair in a big puffy ponytail.

"Hello," Shelby says. "Can we talk to your mama?"

She shakes her head.

"Is she home?"

She shakes her head again.

Just because a kid has a snow day doesn't mean her mother has a day off from work. "How about your father?" I ask.

"He's at prayer."

Right. Friday noon prayer. I check my watch. It's a little after eleven.

"Where?" Shelby asks without my prompting.

She closes the door, and we're left out in the cold.

"There are only two Islamic centers in the area. One is ecumenical—they serve all Muslims. The other is primarily Somali,"

Shelby says.

I raise an eyebrow.

"I did some asking around while I was searching yesterday," she says. She's heading for her car. "I'll bet he's at Umatul Center on 2nd Avenue. I'll meet you there."

"They're not going to let you in," I say as I reach my Jeep.

I don't know why, but the fact that maybe she might need my help feels like a win.

Apparently, I've still got Young Rem in me somewhere.

I drive over to Queen's "Somebody to Love," and park across the street from the center. It's located in a strip mall, the blue awning over the door painted with an orange and red mosque.

Cars jam the parking lot to the side. Shelby pulls up behind me and gets out. "Wait here," I say and head across the street and inside.

Mosques and cathedrals feel the same to me. Quiet, majestic, a desire for the beauty of the building to reflect the grandeur of the Holy. Still, I've never felt particularly close to God standing under the arch of a painted dome.

Instead, for a while, I found him in the wooden pew of our small country church. Just a congregation of eighty, but the preacher made my heart burn every Sunday and I'm sure I went forward on a dozen altar calls.

I'm not sure if that makes me super saved or just desperate, but you know my story. What would you have done in my pitiful shoes?

I haven't exactly abandoned God, nor my desperation. I'm just not sure where to find him today.

The Umatul Islam Center is not a mosque. But it is a building used for prayer. At the entrance, I slip off my shoes. A basket holds extra taqiyah caps, but since I'm not here to pray, I don't grab one.

Instead, I walk into the prayer hall. Covering the floor is a large red carpet, with rows and rows of pillars woven into the design.

Men sit in rows behind these pillars, some of them cross legged, a few of them on their knees. The Zuhr hasn't started yet, but the place is quiet in preparation.

I scan the crowd for Yasir. I don't exactly remember what he looks like—yes, I could pick him out of a small crowd, but this crowd is large—maybe sixty men, and they all wear taqiyahs, most of them white, some multi-colored. Many are in suits, dress pants and shirts, a few in thobes.

"Can I help you, sir?" A man standing near the entrance has approached me. He speaks well, but with an African accent, and is wearing a thobe under a suitcoat, and a gold prayer scarf.

"I'm looking for someone. Yasir Isse."

"I'm sorry, sir, but prayers are about to start."

"I just need a quick, friendly chat." I'm not wearing my badge outside my jacket, like Shelby, and I don't want to pull it out. But the man's eyes flicker down to my chest, as if searching for it, so yes, I pull my coat open. "He's not in trouble," I add.

His mouth pinches.

A few men have glanced our way, and I quickly scan the crowd. But no one looks familiar.

Clearly my presence has the effect of a Labrador to a bouquet of pheasants. In the back, a man rises. Looks at me.

Yasir.

I raise my hand, smile.

He turns and strides—okay, runs—the other direction.

Aw. He's running. Don't run!

I grab my shoes and make a break for it across the carpet, around the back, slipping on my shoes at the back door.

It leads out to the parking lot, which is packed with snow and ice and the last thing I want to do is run out in my stocking feet.

But that didn't stop Yasir. Which means he's not getting far.

I take off through the lot, around the back towards the front, trying not to fall on my face in the snow.

I skid onto the sidewalk and search for him.

Shelby is on the run after him, taking off down the street as he flees in his socks.

The woman can move. I take off after them as he scrambles down the street toward the corner.

He can't run far because on the other side of the snowy bank is the barrier wall to Highway 35W, and maybe he knows this because he cuts away from the highway, through a McDonald's parking lot, and into a berm of snow, heading for the neighborhood beyond.

Shelby catches him as he's trying to climb, his feet plunging deep into the depths, slowing him down.

As she pulls him back, he rounds on her.

"Get down!" I yell, to him, but also to Shelby.

He lunges at her, but she's fast, and dodges him.

He lands on his hands and knees, sees me and puts his hands up. "Don't shoot!"

Yeah, right. I'm not even holding my gun. I walk over and shove him down. "I'm not going to shoot you. I just need to talk to you."

Shelby is breathing hard. Looks at me. "I don't think he meant to hurt me. I think he was falling."

Whatever. "Cuff him anyway."

I have to admit, she's got some steely nerves, because he's calling her names, in Arabic, that I don't understand but can figure out.

"Cork it, buddy," I say.

"You're going to get me and my family murdered." He says,

and glances down the street at the mosque, I'm sure to see who might be watching.

"You're the one who ran."

"I had to run. I can't be seen talking to you."

"Get in the car."

"Not here. You have to take me somewhere."

He's *that* scared. "Okay. Let's go down to the station."

"Are you arresting me?"

"I'm thinking about it." I look at Shelby. "You okay to drive him?"

She nods.

I stand there as she runs to her car and drives it back to pick him up.

My blood is a little hot as I follow her into the city, to a little Foreigner, "Cold as Ice." We pull into the parking ramp and escort Yasir into the building, down the hall to the homicide division, and into an interview room.

It's a plain room, round table, plastic curved chairs.

Shelby uncuffs him—a move I'm not too sure about, but he sits down and runs a hand around his wrists.

"This work for you?" I say and straddle the chair, my arms on the back.

"You're going to get me killed." He glares at me.

I ignore him. "We found your note to Fadima," I say. "At the women's shelter."

He leans back, folds his hands over his suitcoat. He's wearing dress pants and a clean black shirt and a white taqiyah on his dark head. "I tried to warn her."

"Talib is her husband, then?"

He nods, and glances at Shelby. "Did Maryam tell you about him?"

"She didn't get the chance," she says, and her voice has a hardness to it I've never heard. "She seemed pretty scared."

"You try moving to a new country and have everyone think you're a terrorist."

I glance at Shelby. I don't think that's what she meant, but I don't chase it.

"Why did you warn her about him?" I ask.

"Because Talib Mahad is a very bad man," Yasir says. "He beats her, and their children. She ran from him to a refugee camp."

That gives me some pause. If he thinks this, then maybe I read his body language incorrectly at the house.

"How did Talib get here?"

"I want water."

"Sure." I pause, lock my gaze onto his. "Later."

He folds his arms over his chest. "Hassan Abdilhali. Talib worked for him in Somalia, and Hassan made him a promise that he would bring him to the United States."

Oh, terrific. "Did Hassan's promise include helping Talib find his wife?"

"Probably. Or maybe he did that on his own, but when I saw him at prayer, I knew I had to warn her."

I can't figure this guy out. He's a tough guy, not a hero, but then again, he went out of his way to warn his sister-in-law.

"Do you think he found her through you?"

The question hits home. He sighs and unwinds his arms. "Maybe." His jaw tightens. "Yes, probably. She had left, and I didn't realize that Maryam had asked her to pick up our children. He might have followed me home, seen her at our house." He looks down, at his hands. "So, I am to blame for Fadima's death."

My father's words flash through me. *For some devil that showed up on a dirt road and murdered your brother, and tried to steal your soul?*

"You're not responsible for his actions. But you might be responsible for her children's deaths if you know where he is and don't tell us."

"It won't matter." His eyes shift up to me. "You won't be able to get to him."

"Try me."

He leans back then. "He's working out of Hassan's new office. It's located in a container yard and warehouse off Longfellow Avenue. But Talib's probably not there. He's…" He raises a shoulder. "Busy."

And by busy, I am sure Yasir means breaking legs and terrorizing Hassan's employees.

Yasir leans forward now, his hands folded on the table. "Listen. I don't know where the children are," he says, then meets my eyes. "If I did, I would tell you. Maryam is…not well. She left last night to go to her uncle's home in Bloomington to grieve. I promised her I would keep her sister safe, and I could not." He looks at Shelby, then back to me. "I came to this country wanting a new life. But it seems my old one has followed me."

I cannot tell you how much his words hit me. Choices.

He meets my eyes again. His are deep brown, and they hold a sincerity, an earnestness in them.

I believe him.

"Help us find the kids," I say to him. "I know you work for Hassan. Use your contacts to find Talib."

He sighs, his mouth a tight line. "He watches me. All of us. He will know." But then he nods. "Yes. I will do it."

I'm wondering, suddenly, if he might also be the one to help Burke and Danny. I file that information away and hand him a card.

Shelby does the same. "You're free to go. But we could use that wedding picture of him."

Interesting. She's not going to charge him for taking a swing at her.

She doesn't look at me, but I know what she's doing. It's this kind of choice that will help her line up her list of informants on the street.

"Yes. We have a neighbor staying with the kids. I'll call her and tell her to give it to you." Yasir stands up and meets my eyes. "Talib is an evil man. I do not want to lead him to my children."

He's asking me to be careful and I nod.

We escort him to the lobby and call him a cab.

He is standing there, looking out the window at the world that's followed him as we leave.

"I need to call Burke. We might need to pay a visit to Hassan." I say to Shelby as we walk back to my office.

"I'm going with you."

I stop her, my hand to her arm. "No. Swing by Maryam's house and pick up that wedding photo. I'll talk to Eve and see if we can track down the uncle so you can pay her another visit. Ask Maryam if Fadima has any other friends in the area the children might have run to."

Shelby's mouth is a pinched line, but she knows I'm right.

She heads for the door, and I pull out my phone.

Burke answers on the first ring. "Rem."

"I found Hassan's new HQ. It's a warehouse off Longfellow."

"Yeah, we're staked outside it right now."

Of course they are. "Yasir Isse, the brother-in-law of the victim, said that Talib was in the country and working for Hassan. I think he took the kids."

"Okay," Burke says. "I'll tell Danny." He pauses. "See you

tonight?"

The jazz gig. "Yep."

The only thing that matters is right now. What you choose is who you are, and the future you're writing. Get that right and you don't have to worry about the what-ifs.

I head up to the third floor, aware that for the first time in days—which actually means years—I am not dreading what I've done to Eve. Not worried about regret, or shame or feeling like a jerk.

Silas is at his workstation as I enter, looking through a microscope.

"Hey," I say. I'm looking for Eve, but although I see my mother's muffins on her table, she's not around. "Have you seen Eve?"

Silas looks over at me. "She's not here. She's working a case."

"Oh. What case?"

"It's a couple months old. The Delany case, I think. She was going to talk to a tattoo artist about some sketch she made. I think she said Midtown Ink."

I still.

Because if Leo Fitzgerald finds out she's on his trail…

And it occurs to me, then, maybe this is why Ashley was killed. Because Eve and I got too close to Fitzgerald.

C'mon, Eve. Don't mess with time!

CHAPTER 12

Eve could almost hear Rem's voice—*Eve, you're brilliant*—as she pulled up to the Midtown Ink tattoo parlor. He'd said it before, and frankly, she *felt* brilliant.

Like she might be a bona fide investigator.

Not that she wasn't—and she liked lab work— but listening to Rem talk last night about the clues he'd gathered about the Lauren Delany case—clues she'd overlooked—made her want to up her game.

She'd even impressed herself.

First, she'd gone back to the evidence box on Lauren Delany's case and discovered that no, the M.E. had not done a DNA test on the fluids in her body.

She processed the rape kit, and sent out for DNA results.

Then, she drew a picture of the tattoo he'd described and looked up the address and phone number for Midtown Ink.

Yes, Chad Grimes was working.

She left the muffins on her desk and headed out to Midtown Ink.

The place was located just a few blocks from her house, in a small white building off Lyndale not far from Uptown. She parked in front of a cycling shop, closed for the winter, and got out. Two tiny row houses sat between the cycling shop and the building, snow piled on their front porches, plastic over the windows.

A bus pulled up to a stop across the street and at the corner, neon lights suggested a Bud Light at a bar called Smithy's.

Okay, so not the safest corner in town, and the sun was finding its way down the backside of the day, but if she could find Chad, and if he knew Leo Fitzgerald, then Rem would be one step closer to finding Lauren's killer.

Frankly, he had enough on his plate with trying to locate the missing children. At one point, he'd jerked and rumbled in his sleep last night, murmuring, and she thought she should wake him.

But then he'd stopped moving, out like a stone, so he needed his sleep. She had the feeling he didn't sleep much.

She'd slept with the very real awareness of his warm, strong body next to hers. And with the words he'd said ringing in her ears. *But I'm trying to do this right this time.* She didn't exactly know what he meant, but maybe it had something to do with his silence over the past four months.

That, or another woman, but she didn't have the courage to ask him, really. But the fact that he wanted to do things right…

She could fall hard for this man. Probably already had.

She wanted him to call her brilliant. Believe she was in his league.

The shop was open, lights inside. It resembled a barber shop, with chairs and tables set up near workstations. Except the workstations, covered in tinfoil and paper, were stocked with water bottles, inking needle machines, razors, hustle butter, and cups of colors.

The place smelled of ammonia, and soap, a hint of air freshener and along the walls, rows and rows of the artists' work hung as a massive gallery. A twenty-dollar bill in a frame hung over another with a copy of his operator's license.

Tom Petty played on the loudspeakers—Rem and his classic rock music addiction would like this place.

A man sat on a table in the back, one leg outstretched, and sitting in front of him, on a stool, another man bent over him, armed with a needle and a paper towel. The faintest buzzing sound lifted from the depths of the room.

She just stood there, not wanting to interrupt him—what if he made a mistake?—and finally he looked up. "Are you looking for some ink?"

"No," she said, "I'm looking for an artist named Chad Grimes."

The man was burly, bald, and wore reading—or perhaps in his case, tattooing glasses, a black T-shirt and a pair of camo pants. "That's me," he said and got up.

He was big. Over six feet tall, and he spoke with a deep voice that reminded her, oddly, of a Harley engine.

Oh, what was there to be afraid about? "I need to ask you about a particular tattoo." She walked toward the back and pulled out her credentials. "I'm from the Minneapolis Police Department Crime lab, and we're investigating a homicide."

Up close, he smelled a little like sweat, and wore a Fu Manchu beard. But he seemed nice enough as he took her drawing. "Yep," he said. "That's my work." He handed it back to her. "Who are you looking for?"

"A man named Leo Fitzgerald. He is a suspect in the murder of a waitress a couple months ago."

He frowned. "Leo? Naw. He's a good guy. Wouldn't hurt anyone."

"DNA on her body says differently."

He raised an eyebrow. "Who is this victim?"

"A woman named Lauren Delany."

The breath seemed to wheeze out of him, and he turned to the man on the table. "I'll be right back."

Then he gestured her to the front of the shop, cut his voice low. "How was she killed?"

She'd pulled the file, reread it as she pulled the DNA. "She was strangled. Right after she was raped."

He ran a hand behind his head. "Leo wouldn't do that. He loved her. Lauren was his girl. I can't believe he would have hurt her—"

"Maybe they got in a fight. Maybe it boiled over…" She looked around the shop, her gaze landing on a picture of a group of soldiers. "This your unit?"

"Yep." He walked over and took the picture off the wall, handing it to her. "The Big Red One. 1st Infantry. We served together in Desert Storm."

She counted nine of them. "Tough-lookin' crew."

"Yeah. Led by Sergeant Rossi. Big John. Bravest man I know." He pointed to him, and Eve stared at the man. Unremarkable, really, but he wore a smile, his arms around two of his guys. Blond hair, thick around the middle.

"Don't know what happened to him. I heard he was KIA, maybe." He pointed to another face. "This is Leo. He was always a little quiet, to himself. Not a ladies man, but he had a stillness that some women liked."

Leo was blond and tall, wide-shouldered but thin. "Did you give him the tattoo?"

Chad drew in a breath. Nodded. "It's a BRO tat."

BRO. Oh. Big Red One.

"So, did all your squad get one?"

"Not all of them. But I have one too." He raised his short

sleeve and revealed the tat. "I designed it, and it got picked up by a few guys. I've seen fellow BROs all over the country sporting the tat."

Interesting. "Thanks." She looked at the picture again. "Can I take this?"

"Bring it back?"

She nodded. Then, "Do you know where I might find Leo?"

The debate played over his face, brotherhood versus the law.

"We just want to talk to him."

He nodded. "I sometimes see Leo at a bar out in Montrose called The Joint."

"Thank you, Chad. If you see him, would you be willing to call me?" She pulled out a card and handed it to him. "My name is Eve Mulligan."

He tucked it into his pocket then gave her a playful smile. "Sure you don't want any ink?"

"I'm sure. But my brother Sams does. I'll send him your way."

His smile grew and he winked.

Yep, Eve, brilliant.

She stepped out into the street.

"Eve."

She looked up to see Rembrandt striding toward her, his eyes dark. He looked almost angry, his hair rucked up, his coat open, a grizzle on his face and chin. "Are you okay?"

Uh, yeah, but she didn't have time to answer because he took a hold of her upper arms. "What were you thinking?"

She stared at him, then twisted away. "What are you talking about?" And never mind the thudding of her heart, the way his words turned her body to poison.

He was breathing hard and staring at her as if trying to conjure up the words. "You shouldn't be...well...Leo Fitzgerald is dangerous, and you shouldn't be trying to track him down."

"I was going to call you, Rem. What did you think? That I was going to head out to Montrose by myself?"

He drew in a breath. "What's in Montrose?"

"Some bar that Fitzgerald hangs out in. I was going to call you to go there with me—"

"No. Absolutely not. You are not to get within spitting distance of Leo Fitzgerald!" He was nearly shaking, and sort of freaking her out. And maybe he knew it, too, because he ran his hands behind his neck, folded them there, turned away from her.

"Rem?"

"Eve? Everything okay?"

She glanced over her shoulder and Big Chad had stuck his head out of his open door. "Yes. Thanks, Chad." She gave him a smile.

Chad's gaze flickered over to Rembrandt, something wary in his eye.

Rembrandt turned and met his gaze, something of a challenge in it, but then held up his hand. "We're just having a discussion about…" He glanced at her. "Eve's propensity to go off without her *partner*."

Chad nodded slowly. "I was wondering about that." He glanced at Eve. "Okay then. Watch her back."

And suddenly Chad had shifted sides. She half-expected a high five.

"I can take care of myself," she snapped when Chad went back inside.

Rem's mouth made a thin line. Then he reached out and grabbed her hand, pulling her into the alleyway between the shop and the cycle store. It was snowy and dirty and he pushed her against the wall, bracing his hands on either side of her head.

"You shouldn't have gone." he said, his voice low and gravelly, as if wrenched out of dark place. "You're not a cop."

"In point of fact, I am. I went to the Academy. I took the same oath you did—"

"It's not the same!"

His tone made her still, shucked the air out of her body. The man was really scared. She'd never seen that in Rem before—although, maybe a hint of it last summer when the drive-by shooters hit her house, when her mother lay bleeding on the sidewalk. But now, the intensity of it shook through her.

He touched his forehead to hers, as if in prayer. "Please, please, please stay far away from Leo Fitzgerald and this investigation. He's dangerous, Eve."

His soft, broken tone could undo her.

He met her eyes, something almost desperate in them. "He's killed more than one woman, I know it, and he's going to kill more if I don't stop him—"

"We—"

"No." He lifted his head. "*Not* we. You have to promise me you'll walk away from this. Stay in the lab. Please." He touched his bare hand to her cheek. And sure, it was cold, but it sparked a fire through her entire body. "I cannot lose you."

Why would he—

Then he kissed her. And yes, he'd kissed her last night, but it was all reined-in control, something sweet and soft and languorous.

This kiss was all desperation, maybe even possession as he took her mouth, as he practically inhaled her. And yes, she knew Rem, knew the way he lived—intense, full out, dedicated, but to have it directed at her—

As if, yes, he was all in, committed, giving himself over to her.

She softened her mouth, let him kiss her, almost as a catharsis to whatever nightmares raged inside him, tasting in his kiss the things he'd said to her last night. *Eve, there is nothing more—nothing—that I'd like to do right now than...kiss you. No, I don't just want to kiss you. I want to take you upstairs...*

Good thing they weren't at home because she wasn't so sure she'd say no.

He wove his fingers through her unruly hair, held her face and finally leaned away, his eyes hard in hers.

Said nothing as she wrapped her hands around his wrists. "You okay?"

He swallowed, nodded, but his eyes glistened. And she didn't know what had Rembrandt Stone so afraid, but she wasn't going to let his nightmares materialize. "I'll stay away from Leo Fitzgerald."

He pulled her close, his arms wrapped around her, and she felt the thunder of his heartbeat.

"But I expect you to keep me in the loop...partner."

He laughed, and the rumble went clear through her. And when he pulled away, he ran a thumb across his cheek. Then he grinned at her. "So, you got Leo Fitzgerald's address."

"And a picture." She patted her satchel. "And, Chad said that Lauren was not just some random victim, but his girlfriend."

He raised an eyebrow. "Eve Mulligan, this is why you're brilliant."

Yes, yes she was.

CHAPTER 13

The truth of the matter is that I'm already itching for a fight by the time I arrive at The Joint, thirty miles out of the city in a little town called Montrose. It's more of a blink, than a town. Around it, farmhouses sit on fields that stretch as far as the eye can see on the horizon. One stoplight, a convenience store, a bar, a small cluster of newly built homes in a subdivision that will never happen because it's so far out of the city.

The Joint is a dilapidated building and the only other place in town. It has a patched roof and neon lights in the grimy windows. Strangely, at four o'clock in the afternoon on this snow day, the parking lot has been cleared and is full of cars. Pickups, a couple of sedans, one nice looking Lexus that doesn't belong here.

I get out of my Jeep and head inside.

The place is as expected—dingy lights, a long bar, stools, most of them taken by what I assume are locals, or perhaps regulars. A couple farmers dressed in Carhartts, a man in jeans and a pullover shirt, some guys shooting pool in the back, wearing jeans and flannel.

I walk in and sit next to a man in his mid-thirties. Short brown hair, nearly balding. He wears a pair of suit pants and a dress shirt, the sleeves rolled up. Has to be Lexus man. He wears a wedding ring and sips on a beer, watching a rerun of a recent Minnesota Wild hockey game on the flat screen above the bar.

I wonder if he's run away from home. I picture him having three little girls and a wife waiting for him. He probably lives in the subdivision. His beer is about half-empty.

I've taken the picture Eve gave me of the Big Red One squad, scanned it at nearby print shop, enlarged Leo's picture, copied it and now have a fairly decent reproduction in color of the guy I'm hunting.

I figure the picture was taken maybe five or six years ago so he can't look that much different. Leo, from my rough description of the picture, stands around six feet, has blond hair, may or may not wear a beard and sports the tattoo Eve identified.

She is brilliant, I know it.

Maybe I shouldn't have kissed her like that, so much of myself on the outside, but for a second all I could imagine was Leo getting his hands around her neck, and it scared me to the bone. And then, for a moment I was the Rembrandt that I knew, the one with a wife and a daughter, who wrote novels—or tried to—and desperately needed his wife to come home every night to him.

So, I kissed her like the man I was, the man that knew her, the man that needed her. The man who couldn't let her go. And let's just be honest here…I was kidding myself thinking I wasn't going to get involved. I'm way involved, up to my neck in my past life, and I know the price I'll pay when I leave. If Young Rem doesn't get his act together, then I'm still going to break her heart, I'm still going to have my daughter, I'm still going to go undercover and lose everything I have. Because, Eve is right. I am driven, and intense and obsessive and focused and will do anything to take the people off the streets who might hurt the people I love.

That's the man I am, and right now the choice I'm making might cost me my career, but that's who I am right now, too.

I flash the picture of Leo to the guy next to me and say, "Hey, I'm looking for this guy. His name is Leo. Ever seen him?"

The man looks over at me, raises an eyebrow, eyes the picture. "Nope," he says and turns his attention back to the television set.

I didn't really expect a hit on the first try, but I am disappointed.

The bartender has long brown hair pulled back into a ponytail. He walks over to me and sets a coaster on the wooden bar. "What are you drinking?"

I take a chance. "Macallan."

He laughs. "Nope. Just good old Uncle Jack."

Not even close, but I nod. "Add a little soda to it, on the rocks."

He nods. Puts a highball with ice on the counter. Grabs the bar hose and a bottle of whiskey and fills it.

I look at the game. The Wild are up by one. It's not a game I recognize. If it were, maybe I would be able to make a little cash, but I wasn't into sports—except for the Vikings, but that's more of a statewide addiction-slash-malady. If it were Sunday, I might be in luck, but it's a Friday night and if my estimation is correct, I'll be home, and by that I mean *my time*, before the Vikings play.

That seems a long way away from now. Tonight is also the night that two children will burn to death in a house fire, so it's going to be a long night.

I show the picture of Leo to the bartender. "Have you seen him?"

The bartender considers me. "Why?"

I've tucked my badge in my shirt. I don't know why. I guess I don't want to scare him off. We haven't been able to find him in the future, so I know he's good at being in the wind.

More, I'm not sure the evidence against him, right now, despite Eve's investigation, is solid. Eve did say she'd pulled DNA evidence on him, and I know in the future it will match Leo Fitzgerald. That, along with the connection to the victim, and maybe a match to that footprint will be enough to nail him.

Save thirty-eight women.

But I'm not sure, and the last thing I want is for him to run, so, tonight will start with a conversation. A meet and greet so I can get eyes on him.

Although, I do have cuffs on me if things get dicey.

I look at the bartender with an even eye and say, "I know him from the war." It's not completely a lie, is it? Because there is a war going on, one that's in my soul, and in the future.

He nods and glances towards the pool table. "Leo's over there," he says quietly.

Three words that stun me.

I have found him.

I don't take the drink, but I stare at the TV. Glance at the guys in the back. They're setting up for another round of eight-ball, racking the balls. I spot Leo.

He does look different. No beard, his hair is long, pulled back around his ears. He's wearing a flannel shirt, so I wouldn't have noticed the tattoo, and he's got a grizzle, maybe two or three days on his chin. He's a big guy, and he's filled out since his picture, or maybe I should say before his picture. Maybe thirty or forty pounds. He looks like he can handle himself and as he bends over the cue, I notice he has big hands.

He takes the shot, cracks the balls. One of them pockets and he points at it, says something I can't hear to his buddy and laughs.

He takes another shot, misses and steps back.

I pull out a ten and throw it on the counter. Then I walk back to Leo.

He's leaning against the wall, holding the cue with both hands and gives me a look as I walk up to the table.

I put down a dollar. "I'm in next."

Leo takes his cue and flicks the dollar on the floor. "Nope. This is just a game of fun. You're not invited."

I keep my eyes on him as I pick up my dollar and shove it back in my pocket. The other guy takes a shot. He misses.

Leo steps up. I stand back and watch.

He lines up. Then he looks at me. "You want something, mister?" Challenge rakes his voice.

I hold up my hands and step back. I need a little more time to size him up, to figure out how I'm going to do this. And maybe, just a little, I wish I'd called Burke. It's always nice to have a guy watching your back over at the bar.

Leo takes his shot. Pockets the ball. Takes another, misses and steps back. "I need a beer," he says and walks over to the bar.

This could be bad. Because the minute he gets his beer, the bartender is going to ask, "Hey, did you see your friend?" And well, you know what's going to happen after that.

But before I can step between him and the bar, the other guy comes up to me. His voice is low. "What are you doing here, Rem?"

I still and look at him. He has a full head of blond hair, and is tall, over six feet, a little beefy and he's holding out his hand as if he knows me. I meet it, scrambling.

The thing is, usually being from the future has its advantages.

And then there's the moment when you realize that your choices in the past have also changed your history.

"Haven't seen you for a few months. How's your back?"

143

My back. Right, the stabbing wound from the coffee shop. Is he a doctor? "It's good."

"Keep up those stretches. The scar tissue can tighten up, and pretty soon your muscles are all knotted." He clamps me on the shoulder.

"Yeah, thanks." I'm clearly nonplussed and doing a poor job of hiding it.

Which is why, maybe, the man glances at Leo. "Why are you here?"

And the jig is up because behind me I hear the bartender give up the goods on me.

So I turn and say, "Leo Fitzgerald, I need to talk to you about the murder of Lauren Delaney."

Yes, I do understand that maybe I should have thought that out more. That I should have had my cuffs in hand, and backup, but like I said, I'm not doing a great job of thinking this through.

Leo looks at me, frowns. "What?" he asks quietly. "Who are you?"

"Inspector Rembrandt Stone, homicide, Minneapolis Police Department," says my friend behind me.

Oh, thanks, pal. Whoever you are. But I ignore my betrayer and follow quickly with, "I need you to step outside with me, please."

"I ain't goin' nowhere with you, buddy," Leo says and picks up his beer.

"Fitzgerald—"

"I didn't kill Lauren," he snaps. He starts to push past me, gives my shoulder a bump with his.

It's not the bump but the carelessness of his words that looses something inside me. "I didn't say you did," I say carefully.

Like I said, I was itchin' for trouble before I came in, so I should probably back away.

He gives me a suggestion that is physically impossible and pushes past me.

It's almost on reflex that I slip my leg between his. I just want him on the ground so I can cuff him.

He trips, falls forward and is about to go down but grabs himself on the bar. Then he turns, and he's still holding the cue.

Shoot.

I know he's going to swing it at me, so I step back and let it go past me, then grab it and jerk it back. I've surprised him and I yank it from his hands.

He might have been in the military, but I've spent years boxing with Burke every week. I throw the cue aside and step up to him. He's an inch or two taller than me, and bigger, I admit.

But I'm mad.

And he's just startled.

I've been in a number of fights that were serious. I already told you about the one with Burke. There was another fight, back in high school, with a kid who had said something lewd to a girl I liked. She never knew I liked her, but when this guy called her a name, I lit into him and we brawled in the middle of gym class. I left his blood on the basketball court, along with my own and got suspended for two weeks. He never spoke to her again.

And then there was the other time. The one that is still whispered about on the force, that Eve won't let me talk about. But it was after I had found the dead body of a little girl. She'd been raped and murdered and when they identified the father's DNA on her I went out of my mind. Even before they could arrest him, I found him. I'm not going to say anything more about that, except that he didn't die. It wasn't homicide, but a lesson. Doesn't make it right—I know that.

I feel that old lesson stirring up as people step back, and Leo steps forward.

I hold up my hands, probably more for myself than him. "Listen, I don't want trouble—»

He swings at me and I duck.

Not cool. But I back away. "Take a step back, and no one gets hurt."

He laughs.

Laughs. And all I hear is the quiet voice of Hollie Larue saying, *He told me not to scream...*

Then he comes at me again, and even as I block his punch, I land a very solid blow in the center of chest. The air wheezes out of him. He steps back, heat in his eyes.

"Leo—"

He launches at me, so I guess we're getting dirty. He takes me down to the floor and lands a punch in my ribs, another in my gut.

I send an uppercut to his jaw and my fist explodes.

He yells, lunges back and I slam my open hand into his chin to finish the job. He rolls away, and I bounce to my feet.

"You're not going to hurt anybody else. Any other women," I snarl.

His nose is a wreck, his mouth is cut and he's looking at me with wild eyes. "What the hell are you talking about?"

I know exactly what I'm talking about, and he does too. And when he reaches for his pool stick, laying on the floor, I leap at him.

We go down, this time with me on top, and I have my arm against his throat. "Stay down!"

He grabs my ears and pulls.

The pain blinds me and I tear away from him.

He gets up, his grip on the cue and takes a swing for my head.

Home run. I hit the floor, my eyes rolling back, seeing gray.

Sirens burn the air, and darn it, I'm not done with this guy.

I try to find my feet, but the room is woozy, so I grab the bar. "Look out!"

I'm not sure the warning is for me, but I turn and lift my arm just as a chair crashes over me.

I hit my knees, but I roll and put my hands out to stop Leo as he charges.

I grab his arms, knee him in his gut, and throw him off. Scramble to my feet and when he comes back at me, I throw a right cross that I put my whole life into.

He spins around, hits the bar, bounces, and scatters a number of chairs on his way down.

He's on all fours, breathing hard.

I'm breathing hard.

We're both bleeding—I've got blood pooling in my ear. My ribs hurt and I want to vomit. The room is still spinning a little.

He looks up at me. "I didn't kill Lauren. I loved her!"

"I don't call people I love names," I say, my voice low and dark.

He draws in a breath. His body tenses, eyes narrow.

Yeah, that's it. Come at me, pal. Let's finish this.

The bar door slams open. A uniform bursts in. "Stop! Get down."

He points his gun at me.

I'm not sure why except Leo is turned around and I'm the only one standing there with my suit torn, my hands destroyed and my face bloodied.

I fall to my knees and put my hands up. "Do not shoot me! I'm a cop. I'm here to arrest him—"

But when I point, Leo is not there. I look around and I don't see him. I start to my feet.

"Get down!" the cop yells at me. He's a young one and has his gun out and I'm not taking any chances.

"I am a cop," I say. "And I'm here to arrest a murder suspect."

"Yeah? Where's your badge?" he says, and the gun is shaking a little in his hands.

Calm down, pal. "I'm reaching for it—"

"Don't move."

"I'm an investigator with the Minneapolis Police Department, and you're letting my suspect get away." I say it in my fifty-two-year-old voice but I now realize that I probably look as young and inexperienced as the boy holding the gun on me, so I might be in trouble here.

But the bigger issue is that Leo has escaped, probably out the back, maybe even helped by the bartender.

My head is really starting to throb. "I'm bleeding, and I'm going to put my hand on my head, okay?" I do it, holding his gaze. "Now, I'm going to reach for my badge. Slowly."

He watches as I reach into my pocket, and search for my badge. It's not there—it might have fallen out during the scuffle.

Great. "It's not here," I say. "I think it fell out."

"Just sit there," the cop says, who is clearly waiting for backup. I read the name on his badge—Nielson.

The bartender hands me a baggie with ice.

We sit there for a few minutes, and then I hear a familiar voice. I can't believe it when Shelby walks in.

"Put your gun down, officer."

He looks over at her. Her badge is out over her coat. He looks at me and I nod.

I'm not sure why he complies—although admittedly, she sounded a little like she might in a boardroom, selling pharmaceuticals, telling everyone to believe her.

"He's with me," she says to Nielsen as he puts his weapon

away. She walks up to me. Crouches. "You okay?"

The room is still revolving, and my head feels broken in two.

"What are you doing here?"

"Eve sent me."

Eve. Of course she did.

"Did you find him?" Shelby asks. She puts her arm around me and pulls me up from the floor like I'm an invalid. But the room is swimming, so I do grab her shoulder, hold on.

"Yeah, I found him." I glance at the bartender. "You just let my suspect disappear into the wind."

The entire bar grows quiet. Shelby walks up to him and hands him her card, and says, "Call me if Leo Fitzgerald comes back in."

He nods.

"Hey, I found your badge." Lexus man in the suit coat hands me my tin. "Sorry."

And he should be. Because his three little girls need men like Leo off the street. "Thanks," I say.

Shelby turns to Nielson, "I'm taking him to the hospital, and then he'll be glad to file a report for you."

Nielson nods, but we both know I won't be filing any report, and probably Shelby knows this too, because as she gets into her car, leaving my Jeep there, mind you, she shakes her head.

"I know some people out here in the Waconia Police Department. They'll take care of it."

She sounds so much like a seasoned investigator that I really don't know what to say. And I feel like a twelve-year-old boy being chastised by his silent parent as she drives me to the Waconia hospital.

Then she's not so silent. "You should have called me." Her jaw is set. "You want to be partners? Then you have to trust me."

My jaw is tight. "What if I told you that I had a hunch?" I

raise an eyebrow.

"I'm not Burke. You tell me you have a hunch…" She looks back at the road. "I'll believe you."

Huh.

"And, would you have pulled your gun?"

She frowns but doesn't look at me. "He was a cop."

"Let's say he wasn't. And he had me at gunpoint. Would you be able to pull the trigger?"

She swallows, then nods. "Yes. If I believed you were in danger, then yes." Then she glances at me. "I have your back, Rem. Even when you do stupid things."

And now I feel like that unruly teenager again.

I feel even more like it when I enter the ER. I've been here a couple times, but only in high school. Once for a football injury, and once for a homecoming stunt where I might have had a little too much beer and tried to jump a bonfire. Hey, give me a break, I was young and I almost made it.

So, you can see I come by my impulsive, bad decisions honestly. But I'm trying to be a different guy.

"What were you thinking?" Shelby asks as I sit on the end of a gurney and I can't help but sigh at the irony of me asking Eve the same question an hour earlier.

An intern is looking at my wound, and she's waiting for an ER doctor to give me a concussion test.

"I didn't intend to fight him. I just went in to talk to him."

"Without your gun? Your badge? What kind of *talk* was this?" Then Shelby steps back and holds up her hands. "Oh wait. I already know the answer to that." She shakes her head. "A hunch."

Um. Yeah.

The intern picks then to administer the needle of Novocain, and I wince.

"Why didn't you call me for backup?" She wears real hurt in her eyes. "You wouldn't have done this to Burke."

Okay, I'm not scoring high in the works-with-partners-well category right now, and I'm in serious jeopardy of losing this one. So I cut my voice low. "Sorry, Shelby. I just didn't want you to get hurt."

She draws in a breath.

"Any luck on finding the kids?"

"Nope."

With her look, the chastisement bites deep.

I lower my head because not only is she right, but I've lost Leo Fitzgerald.

And then I hear a voice that makes me wince. Because even as the intern is stitching up my wound, even as my head throbs, even as I feel the bruises gathering deep in my body, I know that nothing is going to hurt like John Booker's disappointment.

CHAPTER 14

The fact that John Booker has driven thirty miles out of the city at dusk to dress me down in the middle of a tiny hospital ER should send dread deep into my soul.

But the thing is, Booker knows the truth about me. He gave me the watch, and I'm sure he's wondering what version of me he's going to meet.

The young, reckless me—which, honestly, this looks like—or the older, wiser (sometimes), seasoned investigator he knew before our epic fight that caused me to leave the force.

Epic fight and bone deep fear.

The problem is, along with the watch, he also gave me the rules of engagement, and it's the rules I've shattered that have my throat drying as he walks into the room.

He's wearing a leather jacket, jeans and has his hair cut short, salt and pepper along the sides.

"Chief Booker," Shelby says, more than a little awed by his legendary presence.

"So you're Rembrandt's new partner," he says, and glances at me. I lift a shoulder. "Good luck."

She gives a little laugh, not sure whether he's serious, maybe, and nods.

"Can you give us a moment?" He asks then, and she nods, steps out of the room.

He walks up to me, eyes my wound.

"Pool stick."

"Mmmhmm." He folds his arms over his chest, stands wide-legged. "I don't like getting calls from the Waconia Police Department about how one of our own destroyed a local bar."

"He's a murder suspect. And he started it."

"Are you ten?"

I draw in a breath. Look away.

"Listen, according to Nielson, the cop on duty, he's taken a number of statements that corroborate Fitzgerald started it, so you're off the hook with them." He levels a look at me. "But not with me."

The intern is finished, and she stands up, grabs a Band-Aid and puts it over my wound. "We need to test you for a concussion. So, wait till the ER doc comes in."

The nurse assisting him gathers up the debris. She's pretty, blonde hair, curves. She smiles at me.

For the first time I see her name on her badge around her neck.

Gretchen Anderson.

Wait. I know this name. And I want to tell her to—what?

Stay away from anyone named Fitzgerald?

Not in front of Booker.

She leaves and I turn to Booker. "I don't have a concussion. I'm fine." I grab my jacket ready to slide off the gurney, but Booker puts hard fingers on my shoulder.

"Stay put."

"Chief," I start but he shakes his head.

"We need to talk." His gaze is hard in mine. "Because I need to know if I'm talking to Rembrandt Stone or the other guy."

The other guy, I guess he means, is me. I swallow, look away.

He shakes his head. "I thought so," he says. "I thought we talked about this—you cannot get involved with history."

"This is different, Chief. This is not history. This is an anomaly. This should have never happened."

His eyes narrow a little, and for a second I think I might be in real trouble. Because he's probably knitting my words together and realizing I'm here because I *already* changed something.

He has no idea.

"Okay." He kicks up the rolling chair the intern was in and sits down. Folds his arms over his chest. "Talk."

Huh. "Do you really want to know? Because I don't think you're going to like it."

"Why wouldn't I like it?"

I shrug. "You know, the usual reasons. Here I am, trying to save lives, change the course of history, make things better in the future…"

He rolls his eyes. "We talked about this. You know that if you change one thing it changes a thousand other things."

"Yes. I get it," I say. "Believe me I know. But there's some things that just have to be changed."

"Like what?" he snaps.

Hey, pal, I'm hot too. I still have a lingering punch in me from the Leo brawl, and I add a little of it to my tone. "Like a guy who's going to kill thirty-eight women." I hold his gaze, my eyes steely.

That has him because he takes a breath.

Says nothing. Finally, he gives a slight nod. "I'm listening."

"Years from now, I'm not going to tell you how many, this

guy that I tried to apprehend tonight is good for thirty-eight murders. Mostly working girls, some waitresses, some baristas, some
bartenders. He chases them down, sexually assaults them, strangles
them and leaves a twenty-dollar bill behind as a tip. And the twenties are all marked with the words, *thank you for your service.*"

Booker shakes his head. "That's cold."

"Yes," I say. "Very." I take a deep breath. I'm not sure I should
mention Ashley because then it turns very personal and I have a
feeling his opinion of the situation will change. And I don't, of
course mention that this is the same guy who kills him.

"So, is this guy good for a current crime?"

"He killed his girlfriend a couple months ago. She was a waitress and was found in a Minnehaha Park, raped, strangled with a
twenty in her pocket. When I confronted him today, he said, of
course, that he didn't kill her. They didn't know how she died but
Eve has pulled DNA evidence from her body and matched it to
him." I don't mention that this actually has happened in the future.
But Eve has already pulled the rape kit, and it's on the way.

"What else?"

"There's a shoe print on her back."

"And you think this shoe is from this guy Fitzgerald?"

"It seems like it might be from a hiking boot, or a combat
boot, but of course, we'll have to get his shoes to test it. And, he
has a tattoo. Eve tracked it down to an artist in Minneapolis, and
he identified Leo as the owner of the tattoo. He also gave us the
address of where to find him."

Booker is nodding. "Sounds like solid police work," he says.
"So, what happened?"

I look away. Sigh. "I don't know. A lot of things, I guess. I
didn't call for backup. I didn't tell my partner."

He nods. "Rembrandt, you're smart. You're one of the best

investigators I know. And I'm guessing that I continue to see this, and I continue to trust you, for you to end up with that thing." He points to the watch on my wrist. "And I can certainly understand why, in this case, you came back to stop him. But you break any more rules and I'm going to rethink giving this watch to you. You're reckless, and a rule breaker—although I thought you grew out of that—but you could screw something up and cause Fitzgerald to vanish."

I'm not sure that hasn't already happened, but he's right, so I nod.

"But," he says, and pauses, studying me. "That isn't the case that brought you back."

I frown. "How do you know that?"

"Because if it were, we would be having this conversation two months ago. The watch only brings you back to the moment of death for the victim."

Right. I think I must have worked that out already, but maybe not.

"Who's our victim that you're really here for?"

I don't say it, but of course, it's Burke. Burke and the two children that are missing.

"A woman named Fadima Mahad. She was shot outside her sister's home yesterday morning and her two children went missing. In my timeline, they're found in an abandoned building trapped in a fire and burned to death."

Booker winces. "You're in a race to find them."

"And to solve her murder, which I think I have. Her husband Talib. He's an immigrant from Somalia, I'm not sure if he's here legally or not, but we traced a bullet found in her car to a gun used in a crime a couple weeks ago in the Phillips neighborhood at a gas station. We think it's one of Hassan Abdilhali's men."

"The Brotherhood," Booker says.

"Yes."

"Did you tell Danny Mulligan?"

I nod.

He looks at me now, frowns. "About four months ago, we had a talk about Danny. And a shooting…his wife was shot."

I nod, my mouth a tight line.

"I'm taking a guess that didn't happen the first time around."

Again, a nod.

He gets up and kicks the stool back towards the table. "You're really making a mess of things, aren't you?"

"Trying not to."

He puts his hands in his pockets as if he's considering something. I know to wait for Booker because he's like a strange great uncle, the kind that shows up and says something pithy, changes your life and leaves. He did that throughout my childhood. After my brother disappeared Booker was on the case and he would show up now and again to check on our family. I followed him like I was a young Jedi knight and he Obi-Wan. Our roles have changed now, mostly because of the fight he doesn't know about.

My feelings war inside me.

I love this man. This mentor. The uncle he was to me.

And yet, the fact he doubted me has left a deep, festering wound.

Sometimes it almost feels like hate.

Hate for doubting me. For calling me a coward. For not understanding why I left the force.

And maybe hate that he gave me this cursed watch. So far, I've lost my daughter, opened the door to a serial killer, and last I knew, my wife is married to someone else.

I have seen my parents lives repaired, however, and that is

worth something to me.

I guess hate is a strong word.

I wait and he finally says, "So, how are you?" And I know he's not talking about me now. But me, later. As in tomorrow. I look him in the eyes, not sure what to say.

Finally, "I have a life. I have a wife and a daughter. I have a career."

"Are you still on the job?" And it's funny he should ask that because I would assume that *he* would assume I am.

I think of my recent timeline. "I guess I am." It's really all jumbled up, isn't it?

He smiles. Razor thin, but it's there. "Be stalwart," he says and then he leaves.

And I am left there with the words on the back of my watch now in my head.

Be stalwart. It means loyal and reliable and hard-working, and I'm brought back to the words my father said about becoming the man I want to be.

Choices.

I'm grabbing my coat when the door opens again, and although I expect Booker, or maybe the intern, I'm stilled by the sight of Eve walking into the room.

She's come straight from work, and her hair is pulled back haphazardly into a messy bun. Worry films her hazel green eyes as she walks right up to me and grabs me by the lapels.

"I heard about it. My father called me and said you were in a fight at a bar in Montrose." She pauses. "Did you get him?" Her question is soft and oh, how I love this woman for not commenting on my cut face or the fact that my clothes are dirty and ripped. "Did you get Leo Fitzgerald?"

I take her hands into mine and shake my head. "He got away."

159

Her mouth forms into a thin line. "We'll find him Rembrandt," she says. "I promise we'll find him."

I gather her close to me, my head against hers and hold her for a long time. Finally, "Would you like to go out with me?"

She leans back. "What?"

"Burke has a gig tonight, and he's invited me to it. And I'd really like to see you in a dress."

I know I'm pushing it. But she has great legs.

She rolls her eyes. "What time?"

"Seven? I'll pick you up." I take her hand. "But first, can you drive me back to the bar? I need to pick up my Jeep."

"If it will keep you out of trouble, then yes."

"There are no guarantees," I say but she's ignoring me, and that's for the best. Because like I said, the night is young.

And saving Burke is next on my list.

Like I already told you, this is going to be a long night.

CHAPTER 15

She could not fall in love with Rembrandt Stone this easily.

This easily or this quickly or this completely.

Eve didn't know what had happened over the last twenty-four hours, but she'd gone from wanting to say goodbye to a guy who at best seemed like a stray in her life, to her standing in front of her full-length mirror trying on dresses. Trying on *dresses*. What on Earth had gotten into her? And it was more than just the cozy night before the fire, more than the kiss in the alley, although that went a long way toward losing her heart to him. But when she walked into the ER and saw him sitting on that table, banged up, his clothes torn and dirty, a look of wretched frustration on his face, her heart went out to him.

Then he looked up at her. And so much filled his eyes it took her breath away. Hope. Maybe even relief. And she just couldn't chastise him for his fight—not when he tried to find a killer. So she'd walked over, he'd given her the terrible news, and then he held her.

No. Held *onto* her.

Yes, that was the moment she knew she was desperately in love with Rembrandt Stone.

Then he'd asked her out for dinner, or a jazz festival or whatever. She couldn't really remember the details, just that he asked her if she'd wear a dress.

She owned exactly three dresses. The summer dress that she wore for her father's birthday party Memorial Day weekend. The little black dress she'd used a few times, mostly for funerals. And then there was the long-sleeve flare dress that reminded her of something out of the '70s with blousy sleeves and a paisley print. She didn't know why she bought it, but it smoothed over her body, highlighting all of her curves and with a jacket and a pair of tall boots it could work.

Eve stood looking in the mirror, pulled up her hair, held it there and let it fall back. It was useless. Her hair was a mop that she hadn't a clue how to tame. She'd put on some lipstick and some makeup, however, and maybe the place would be dark. It wasn't like Rembrandt hadn't seen her in her worst clothes. Once he'd come over while she'd been painting. She'd worn a pair of old shorts and a T-shirt, probably wore smudges of paint on her face and yet he'd still kissed her.

So, this was an improvement.

Outside the night was dark, the clocks already falling back to save daylight. Her house lights played upon the snow. Still crisp and white, the night felt a little bit magical.

Oh, she was a stupid romantic.

Especially since, and she didn't know why, but despite all the signs, she wasn't sure Rembrandt had romance on his mind. He'd been deathly quiet when she'd driven him to pick up his Jeep, after he called Burke and asked him for an update.

He'd hung up, told her that the kids were still missing and looked out the window, his jaw tight.

When she dropped him off, he thanked her and told her he'd pick her up at seven.

He didn't go back into the bar but got in his Jeep and headed back to the city.

On her bedside stand, her phone rang. She picked it up.

"Hey Eve," said Shelby.

They seemed to have made a sort of peace yesterday when Shelby dropped off the Arabic note that Eve had gotten translated. She didn't know why but something had shifted between them.

Now Shelby's voice was hesitant. "Rembrandt called and said you guys were going to a jazz club tonight. He said Burke was going to be playing and wanted to know if I wanted to go."

Eve stilled. Really? Again, maybe not a date. So why the dress?

"Um…"

"The thing is I just want you to know that I don't have a thing for Rembrandt," Shelby said. "He's a great guy and, of course, he's my partner, so really, he's off limits, but I know I was…well, I shouldn't have hinted that there was something between us. I'm sorry. I was just angry that you were spending time with Burke and well, I like Burke."

Eve had nothing. Because despite their years as friends, Shelby hadn't once, you know, *apologized*. "Shelbs, Burke and I are just friends."

And she didn't know why saying that suddenly took the what-ifs out of her heart.

Just friends.

Because, you know, she was in love with—

Nope. Nope. Too fast.

"I was wondering if I could take Rembrandt up on his offer and meet you guys at the club."

Eve couldn't put a finger on why it hurt that Rembrandt had

called Shelby. Unless, of course, he was trying to set Shelby back up with Burke.

Now the guy was a matchmaker? Apparently, he had to fix everything from homicides to broken hearts. She supposed she could give him a few points for that.

"Sure. Of course."

"Great. I'll see you there," Shelby said and hung up.

And maybe Rembrandt was in the business of fixing friendships too. Huh.

Although, what if this wasn't really a date? She didn't know what his other agenda might be, but…no, she was simply being paranoid.

She went downstairs. A chill pervaded her house, although the heat was back on.

Maybe Rembrandt could come back here tonight and build her another fire—

Stop.

Let it go. But another part of her wanted to continue what had happened in the alleyway. To bring him home and oh…

Shoot.

Just when she thought she understood the man, Rembrandt Stone turned on a switch and became the stuff of novels.

A knock came at her door, right on time, and Rembrandt stood there, hands in his pockets. "Hey."

He'd showered and changed clothes. He wore a pair of jeans and a leather jacket, his collar up, a scarf, gloves and hiking books. Strange attire for a jazz club, but she didn't hate it. He'd shaved which meant he also smelled good.

He stepped inside and gave a low whistle, which slid under her skin in a soft, dangerous rumble. "You look…wow."

"Thanks," she said.

He opened her closet and grabbed her scarf and jacket, then held the jacket open for her like a real gentleman. She slipped it on.

He looped her scarf around her neck, and for a second she thought he might kiss her. Or maybe she only hoped it. "Where are we going?"

"A small club off Lake Calhoun called The Nebraska."

"I've always wanted to go there."

"Really?" He held open the door for her.

Outside, the night caught her breath, the stars overhead winking. Rem gave her his arm as they walked down the steps.

So maybe it was a date. She needed to stop overthinking this. Just because their last two dates had been pizza and beer...

"Yes. Silas was going to take me for my birthday."

"Of course he was," Rembrandt said. Then he held open her door.

She frowned as he shut it. But maybe he harbored the same feelings about Silas as Silas did him.

"How is Silas?" Rem asked as he got in the driver's side.

Why ask? He'd seen him only yesterday. "He's fine. He's dating a teacher from Minnetonka. She's sweet."

"Good," he said and sounded weirdly relieved.

The Jeep was warm—he'd left it running.

"Any news on the kids?" she asked as they drove around the city.

He shook his head, glanced at her and said, "But I think we'll find out something soon." Words of hope, but the way he said it, so much dread and grimness in his voice that she just nodded.

Because he was probably right. The kids were probably already dead either from the cold or some other terrible thing that had happened to them.

As if he could read her mind, Rembrandt reached out in the

darkness and took her hand, squeezed it. "Thank you for your help with Leo today. You really broke open the case for me."

It was a kind thing to say considering the fact that she'd sent him out to get himself whooped.

The Nebraska was located in a former supper club that overlooked one of the smaller lakes outside Minneapolis. Light gleamed in kaleidoscope against the lake, and from inside, music filtered out.

Rembrandt opened the door and they went inside to the bricked foyer.

They dropped off their coats at a coat check and headed deeper inside.

She expected something quaint and old. Instead, the place had been overhauled with hardwood flooring, two tiers of seating that curved around a massive dance floor and stage.

"I reserved us a booth," Rembrandt said and pointed to one of the rounded booths tucked into the wall along the main floor edge.

She'd stepped onto a movie set.

Already, the band had started to warm up. A grand piano, a man on the sax, a trombone, a bass guitar. Eve spotted Burke sitting behind the drums. He wore a pair of dress pants and a sweater and was working the drum set.

"I didn't know Burke played the drums."

"Yep," Rem said, then gave his name to the maître de. He showed them to their table. "For as long as I've known him. I think it's a kind of therapy."

She got that. Sort of how she felt about remodeling.

People were already seated at tables, waiters bringing drinks and appetizers.

He slid in opposite her. "Uh, by the way," he said. "I invited Shelby." He made a face. "I hope that's okay." He glanced at Burke.

"I thought that maybe she and Burke need to talk."

She nodded. "Shelby called me and asked if she could join us."

He released a breath. Then he met her eyes and said, "There will be nothing between Shelby and me, ever. I promise."

A strange tingle went through her at the man's ability to read her mind. "I know," she said. But really, she didn't, so she let his words sink in and take root.

The waiter came over. "Wine?" he asked her.

She nodded.

"A Black Muscat, I'll bet."

Again, weird. How did he do that? She nodded and he ordered for her.

Rem turned in the booth and looked at the stage, lifted his hand. She followed his gaze and noticed Burke smiling at them. He nodded in greeting.

Rembrandt looked back at her. "I sometimes call him Sticks. He loves the drums."

"He's never mentioned it. We hang out, but he doesn't really talk much about himself." She never really thought about that, but yes, Burke was quiet. Sincere, deft and able, there was a preciseness about him that complimented Rembrandt well. For all of Rembrandt's bold ideas, Burke was the one who could take them apart and analyze about them. It was too bad they weren't partners anymore.

"He's a pretty private guy." He looked over at Burke again. "But he's my best friend, and I'm going to try to go to more of his gigs." He said it more to himself than her, it seemed.

Something caught his eye and he looked past her towards the door and lifted his hand again. "Shelby's here."

She turned and Shelby walked into the room. She wore a pair of black dress pants and a white sweater. Her blond hair back.

Shelby defined sleek and classic and compared to her, Eve felt like a scribble.

Rembrandt got up. "Hi."

Then he glanced at Burke. Eve followed his gaze again and Burke was staring at Shelby, an enigmatic look on his face.

Interesting. Again, Eve couldn't get past the idea that tonight was something very much other than a date.

A waiter came and he ordered shrimp cocktail. "This okay?"

"I love shrimp cocktail," Eve said, narrowing her eyes. "Admit it. You talked to my dad, didn't you?"

"Are you kidding me? If your father knew I was out with you, he'd be staked out across the room." He smiled, his blue eyes warm.

Oh boy.

"Any news on the kids?" Shelby asked, and Rembrandt shook his head. "I feel a little guilty coming out tonight when they're out there in the cold."

The look on Rem's face said he thought the same way. "Danny was staking out the warehouse with Burke today, and said Talib didn't show up. He's in the wind."

They said nothing as the band started up.

Admittedly, Eve had never been a big jazz fan, her dad's Steely Dan records being her closest encounter.

This was not Steely Dan.

This was a long drink of scotch on a hot summer night, the saxophone gentle and smooth, the piano soft, in slow runs and chords, the bass pinging in her bones, and the drums deep, with occasional tinging of the high hat. Burke played with his eyes closed some of the time, not looking at the audience, clearly folding himself into the music.

She recognized the song—"Fly Me to the Moon"—only it was languid and heavy.

Rembrandt looked over at her a couple times, grinning, and his head bobbing.

Oh, why wasn't she sitting with him on the other side of this seat instead of next to Shelby? She would be cozied up to him and there she went thinking about, well, more than just this night.

What would it be like to love this man? The thought had stirred deep inside her as she walked into the ER and now it bloomed as he moved his head to the music. Maybe Rembrandt was not so much of a mystery anymore.

Or maybe she'd just put together the pieces. Justice, drive, loyalty, but also a softer side.

The kind of side that cared enough for his friends to attend a gig.

Her father had stopped complaining about him after Rembrandt had showed up at their picnic and saved his life. And yes, her mother had been injured but, no doubt if there had been two of Rembrandt Stone, he would have tried to protect her mother as well.

Which led her to the reckless over the line side of Rem. Could she love a guy who took her heart into highspeed chases and dark bars, or, God forbid, he went undercover and she didn't know where he was for days or months…or years.

The song ended and switched over to another familiar tune. "Someone to Watch Over Me"…she was humming as Rembrandt looked over at her. A little smile creaked up one side. Wow, he was handsome. And dangerous, especially when he slid out and then leaned over the table.

"Eve—c'mon and dance with me."

She froze. Dance? "I don't know how to dance to this—"

"Come on," he said softly. "Just follow my lead. It's easy."

Easy? Shelby looked at her, almost a dare in her eyes. *Come on, Eve.*

Did she even have a choice? Rembrandt still had his hand out. She slid out and took it and let him lead her to the dance floor.

He pulled her into his arms, put his arm around her lower back. Then he took her right hand with his left, and tucked her right against his body.

And oh, my. If she thought she'd have a hard time keeping her hands off him last night, the feel of his muscular legs beside hers, his strong arms...

"Just move with me. There's a beat and we're just going to follow it. One two, three four. I'll lead, you just relax. That's all there is to it."

No, there was much, much more, and she prayed she didn't fall over. But she wrapped her hand around his bicep.

"I'm just going to hold on."

"Yes, please," he said, his voice at her ear. And then they began to move.

He swayed them on the floor, and he kept it easy. Occasionally he'd step out and make her step back, or step back and make her step forward. He changed up beats after a bit. From every fourth beat to every second beat and then he gave her a little push and lifted his arm and twirled her out. She laughed as he pulled her back in.

"You're good at this. How did you learn?"

"I took a few dance lessons," he said, again into her ear.

She guessed it might be from his mother, but she didn't ask.

A few other couples had joined them, and he continued to move them around the floor.

She could melt into a freakin' puddle right here. And, she didn't know when she'd felt so safe, which was a little strange because Rembrandt Stone was *anything* but safe.

He was dangerous to her heart in every way, and it rattled her how much he put himself out there.

Yes, she was falling for Rembrandt Stone, and she just knew the landing was really going to hurt.

CHAPTER 16

Eve is looking at me like I hung the moon and I am a jerk because you and I both know I'm just here to keep an eye on Burke. And sure, I certainly meant every move I made on the dance floor with Eve. So yes, it's a date but it's also an opportunity for me to save Burke's life.

To intercept him and keep him from showing up at one particular house fire at 10:43 p.m. And I feel a little bit sick that there may be children there. So, here's the plan. At 9:45 p.m. I'm going to slip out of this booth, leave the ladies in Burke's capable hands, and I'm going to go drive over to 17th Avenue in Powderhorn Park and save those two children before the fire starts.

Before Burke can show up.

No fight, but no scars, either.

It's been on my mind all night, of course, especially when Shelby walked in and told me no one had found the kids, adding that she was a little sick about going out tonight. Me too, especially after Eve dropped me off today. I called Burke, and he told me he hadn't seen Talib either.

I drove by 17th Ave and checked the house again. Call me a

little bit crazy and maybe the neighbors do too, but again, no one was there.

It was a little bit more challenging to get into the front door, thanks to the snow. But the kids weren't there and maybe they won't be there at 10:43 tonight, but I'll be there, just to make sure.

Then I stopped by a bookstore, went back to my apartment, changed and left myself a little note inside the book. *Write in me.*

I'm sure hoping young me isn't all spit and vinegar, has a little of better me seeded deep inside.

Although I can admit I like how young me shines up. I look good in a pair of black jeans, a suitcoat.

Now, while I wait for the night to unfold, I'm sitting here with Eve and she, too, looks good. She has great legs like I mentioned, even more amazing eyes and it was all I could do to pry us off the dance floor because I could stay there all night holding her close, seeing the laughter in her eyes when I spun her around and back.

Burke is on stage and he's looked at me a couple of times with a raised eyebrow at Shelby's presence, but I need somebody here to take care of Eve when I leave because I don't know what Burke is going to do. And yes, of course, I want Burke and Shelby to get together, but that's not why I'm here and I'm trying hard not to play with time.

Really.

Yeah I hear you, we both know that's a game I'm going to lose.

So now I'm sitting in the booth, finishing off my dinner of duck confit when the music stops, and Burke's band breaks their set. I glance at my watch. It's 9:00. They're probably going to have another set, so maybe my plan will work.

He comes walking over to us, twirling his sticks.

"Hey," he says.

I look up at him. "You sound good up there."

"Thanks." He looks over at Shelby. "You have room for me?"
She beams. Of course she does. He scoots in.

"I haven't eaten. What's for dessert?" he asks.

"I'm ordering a Baked Alaska," Eve says.

I can tell she's wooed by this night. And I didn't mention it, but she's the one who taught me how to dance. We attended a few of Burke's gigs back in the day and she longed to go out onto the dance floor. So for our first anniversary, I took her to Arthur Murray dance classes and made a fool out of myself for six months while I learned how to not trip over my own feet. But then we got pretty good. And now when we cut a rug, if she leaves, there's a lineup of ladies waiting to dance with me. We can swing dance West Coast, East Coast and foxtrot, waltz and yes, blues dance. Which is really more like swaying to the music, which we did in high school, but I add a little flair to it now and again. Eve isn't quite ready for that yet, but she will be some day.

The waiter comes over and Eve orders her Baked Alaska and Shelly orders flourless chocolate cake. I order coffee. Burke asks for a Coke, leans back and amazingly stretches his arm out over Shelby.

"I can't believe you made it," he says. "I heard about your dust up today in Montrose. What were you doing there, anyway?"

Eve glances my way then answers for me. "He was chasing the suspect."

"Oh really?" Burke says. "Which one?"

"The Lauren Delany case. Remember her? A waitress. We found her at Minnehaha Park."

Burke nods and I'm glad to see that he was still with me at the time because I wasn't sure. "We found that twenty on her, marked up with words."

"Yes," I say. "*Thank you for your service.*"

Eve looks over at me. "That's funny. I saw a twenty-dollar bill just like that today over at the tattoo shop."

I freeze. "What?"

"Yeah, there's a twenty on the wall at the tattoo shop. I didn't ask about it. I thought it was like a memento or something from a customer. It was there hanging right above his picture of his squad. I gave it to you, remember?"

"What squad," Burke asks.

"They're from The Big Red One," Eve says. "A military squad that Chad Grimes and Leo Fitzgerald both served in. That's how I got the name of Leo's hangout place, the bar in Montrose."

Burke looks at me. "Leo Fitzgerald?"

"Yeah, he's the guy I think is good for the murder." I don't know how much he knows and I hope he doesn't feel left out again.

"We've pulled DNA from her—"

"Although I haven't gotten the results back yet," Eve says quickly.

"Too bad you didn't get his DNA while you were slugging him at the bar today," Shelby says.

Thanks for that, Shelby.

But yes, that would have been a better strategy.

Next time. And there will be a next time, because I know where he'll be, and when. I'll simply go back to Lauren Delany's murder and start this over.

Leo is not getting away.

But tonight is about Burke and the two children.

"Apparently Lauren was his girlfriend," I add.

"I found that out too," Eve says.

I really hope that Baked Alaska gets here pretty soon.

"Really," Burke says and looks at Eve. "She's your new partner?" He winks, but Shelby makes a face.

"No, I am," she says. Looks at me. "When did you find this

out about Leo Fitzgerald?"

Oh no, now I'm in big trouble. "I've been working the case on the side a little bit."

By the purse of her lips, Shelby doesn't like this.

She looks at Burke and he shrugs. Apparently, now they have something in common. I'm a bonding experience. Fabulous.

The Baked Alaska shows up as does Burke's Coke, my coffee, and Shelby's cake. Burke takes a sip of his drink.

"Well, I also heard he got away."

I nod. "Yeah. But I'll find him again." And I will. I have a plan, like I mentioned. I can't save her, according to Booker, but I do know where Leo hangs out, and next time I'm not going to be quite as stupid. Leo will go down for the crimes that he will not have committed yet.

The benefits of time travel.

"I didn't know you played the drums," Shelby says to Burke.

"Yeah," he says slowly. "I…" He looks up at me. "Well, I don't usually invite people to these gigs. I kind of like to keep my work life and my private life separate."

She's a little bit crestfallen and turns back to her food.

"But I'm glad you're here," Burke says quickly. "I guess I thought you two would be out looking for those kids." He shakes his head. "I'm sorry we couldn't find Talib today. We staked out the warehouse and followed up on a couple of other leads, but nothing. Danny said he might go back out though."

Burke looks at Eve. "Your father never stops working. He reminds me of Rembrandt."

He smiles but I don't. Because last thing I want Eve to think is that I'm some sort of workaholic. Which apparently, I turn out to be in this timeline, but I'm going to fix that.

"No," I say, "I know when to stop work." Just in case Eve

needs to hear it.

"Yeah, well, on a night like this when it's going to drop down into the teens again, I'm glad Danny is still looking," Burke says. "I should have stayed out there too."

And now I feel like a real heel, but I am going to find those kids. I glance at my watch again. It's 9:20. I'll leave soon.

"I hate the thought of him sitting out there in the cold," Burke says, running his thumb along the top rim of his highball. And I'm remembering now the intensity with which he fought me when he tried to get into the house, so many years ago tonight. "My mom and dad used to leave me alone sometimes on weekends. They'd go out drinking and they wouldn't come home for a day or two."

I didn't know this about Burke. He's turning his glass of Coke slowly.

"When I was nine years old my dad came home one night, drunk. He and my mom had a terrible fight. That was the first time that he ever went to jail, but I was so scared I hid under my bed. It was a cop who found me. I don't know how he knew I was there, but he climbed down onto the floor and looked under the bed. He saw me laying there and said, 'Come on out, kid. You're okay'. And I don't know—it was something about his voice, how calm it was and quiet and sure, that I trusted him. I came out and he picked me up and he put a blanket over my head and then he walked me out of the house so I couldn't see the damage my father had done to my house, and my mother. She was hospitalized for a couple weeks after that. They finally got her to press charges and my father did his first two-year stint, but then he got out and she took him back and…" Burke shook his head. "So anyway, I hope those kids are okay."

I sit unmoving. I didn't know this about him. I mean, yes, I knew he grew up in an abusive home and I know some later stories about how he and his dad went a few rounds before he joined the military, but I didn't know this particular story. And now something is clicking with me because *no wonder* he went a little crazy when those kids burned. I wonder if he sees himself as that cop that found him under his bed. Probably. Burke is the kind of man to do that sort of thing.

"Wow," Shelby says and puts her hand on his arm. He doesn't flinch or shrug it away and glances at her with a tight smile.

Then he looks at me. "I was thinking," he says quietly. "Danny thinks someone should go undercover and try to infiltrate Hassan's Brotherhood." He meets my eyes, something resolute in them that I recognize. "I think I'm going to do it."

C'mon, Burke. No. It's exactly this undercover gig that will steal his life, just like it did mine. I take a breath. "I don't know if that's a good idea."

Burke frowns at me, but I'm not stopping. "It's going to cost you so much of your time, your *life*. It could be months—even years before you—"

"What are you talking about? You're always saying how much you want to go undercover."

"I was wrong."

Even he blinks, because honestly, those are three words I don't say as often as I should.

Then. Now, Eve has taught me the pricelessness of humility.

And it's this old Rembrandt he needs now. "The sacrifice is too great."

"What are you talking about? That's the job, isn't it? Sacrifice for the sake of justice?"

I'm trying to find the right words as I smooth the napkin on the table.

"Yes. But…" I steal a glance at Eve. "I just don't know if it's worth it anymore."

Silence. And Eve takes a breath.

I feel my heartbeat skip, as if time, right then, readjusts.

"Listen," Burke says quietly. "I'm the only one who can do this."

I puff out a long breath. Meet his eyes. "Then, if you go, I'll have your back."

I'm not sure why I said that, right? But maybe I'm tired of the fight between us. "But, just think about it."

He nods, finishes up his drink. "Our next set is starting."

I want to tell him that everything's going to work out. That I'm going to go rescue those kids and he's going to be safe. And that we're going to get Hassan, somehow, without destroying our lives.

I glance at my watch. 9:37.

Shelby's phone buzzes. She pulls it out, frowns and answers it. But I'm turning to Eve. "I have to go," I say.

She is looking at me like I've spoken Russian. "What?"

And I haven't thought this through because of course she's going to be hurt, and confused and...

"Leo's back," Shelby says, hanging up. "That was the bartender from the Montrose bar. Leo is back."

What?

But before I can respond, Burke's phone also buzzes. He pulls it from his pocket and answers it. "Danny?"

And deep inside the back of my brain, there are sirens going off. I've overwritten time so many times who knows if the same things happen again, at the same time, in the exact same way, and written on his face is an expression that tells me my plan has gone south.

"Yes," he says, "on my way."

No! No he won't—but he hangs up. "Sorry. I have to go.

Danny has tracked down Talib. And he's got the kids."

And you know I don't want to say it, but I. Knew. It. His mouth tightens, maybe expecting it.

Instead, I stare at him. My heart's racing because I know history has kicked me sideways, hoping I'll drop out of the game.

Not a chance.

"It's at that abandoned house we were at, right?"

He frowns, "Yeah. How'd you—"

"Just a hunch," I say, not caring.

He looks at Shelby, then Eve. "Sorry to cut this thing short ladies. Thanks for coming out."

I get up. "I'm going with you."

He looks at me, frowns. "What? No, that's okay. You don't need to do that."

"Yes, I do," I say and there's so much urgency to my voice that Eve looks over at me.

"No, you don't. My dad is perfectly capable of taking care of this."

I know she's right, but the fact is that no one can stop Burke from going into that house but me. Nobody knows who he is and what he's been through and nobody knows how hard he hits. I have to be the one. "I'm so sorry Eve," I say. "I have to go." I look at Shelby. "Can you take Eve home?"

She stares at me, a look of confusion on her face, but she nods.

I grit my teeth. And I know I'm crazy because here I am leaving Eve after she looked at me like I hung the moon, after she danced in my arms and I *am* going to be the guy she needs, but right now I have no choice, I have to be the guy Burke needs. Even if he doesn't know it.

He's gone, having disappeared backstage to inform his band. I'll beat him to the scene.

"Rembrandt!" Shelby has run after me, and now she grabs my hand, even as I'm retrieving my coat. "Are you serious? We're just going to leave Leo—"

"Yes," I say. And of course, this is the way fate plays it. Because it likes to play games with me and my life. And if it's not screwing up my future, it's screwing up my present.

"I don't understand. I thought you wanted this Leo guy. He might disappear and it might be weeks before we find him again."

Years, maybe. And I know she's right. In fact, there's a big part of me that agrees with her. That I should hightail it out there, grab this chance. Eve is behind her, gaze locked onto me, her forehead etched with a frown.

And right now, my father's voice pings in my head, and wouldn't you know it, emerges with the truth. *Your choices are the only thing you can control. You have to let go of the rest.*

"Shelby," I say. "We'll get him. I promise. But right now, I have to go help Burke."

Her mouth tightens. And I realize it's not enough.

I have a choice—I can trust my partner. Or I can let fate win.

So, "Listen, Shelby. I know this sounds like a hunch, but I know things. I know if I don't help Burke, and probably Danny," and I shoot a look at Eve when I say this, "will die. Or at least be seriously injured. And I can't let that happen if I have the power to stop it. So, you gotta trust me. Because you're my partner, right?"

Her eyes are wide but she gives me a tight nod. "Okay."

"Good. Please, make sure Eve gets home safe."

And, then, because I'm not sure who I'll be after tonight, I walk up to Eve and kiss her. Something firm and resolute and exactly the kind of kiss from the man I want her to remember.

I might even call him stalwart.

CHAPTER 17

I know you think I've forgotten that Danny Mulligan dies in this fire. I haven't forgotten. That truth throbs in the back of my brain. But I've also been thinking maybe fate has decreed that Danny will die, no matter what I do, and I can't beat it.

I'm clearly not as smart as I hoped.

But, I told you, even before we started, there are no happy endings, and maybe saving Burke is the best I get.

Still, this isn't over, and I call 911 on my way to the house, trying to hedge my bets.

Smoke is billowing out of the back of the house—I can smell it, but can't see it as I pull up.

I get out and hear shouting—both Burke and Danny's voices as I run up to the snow-laden front porch.

So, everyone is still alive. Fate hasn't won yet.

Burke has beaten me to the house, but maybe not by much. I peek inside the front door and despite the darkness, I spot Burke's shadowy bulk crouched down near a doorway.

Gunfire comes from the kitchen.

I don't see Danny anywhere, but I hear swearing and when

gunfire flashes from the stairway, I spot him.

He's hurt. He's holding his leg, and the report of his death pulses in my memory—a gunshot wound. I wonder if he's unable to escape the burning house.

As for Burke, maybe he's burned trying to save his partner.

I don't know what went down.

But I also know that so far, the place isn't engulfed.

Which means we still have time.

I draw my weapon and head around back, through the snow, to the entrance I saw earlier. It's just off the kitchen, so whoever is shooting at Burke—and my educated guess is it's Talib—I'll get the drop on him.

The back door is wedged shut with the snow, so I kick a pathway and wrestle with the door.

It's not quiet and a shot rings out and shatters the window next to me.

I duck down and wish I'd brought my radio.

But then it's quiet.

"Talib!" It's Burke's voice. "You're surrounded. Come out, and this ends. Your kids sleep in a warm, safe place tonight."

Maybe Burke believed me, maybe he's bluffing, but yes, Talib is surrounded. He fires another shot, this time away from me and I jerk open the door and dive inside.

A shot in my direction chips off wood from the flimsy wall. I have my service weapon out, a Glock 22, and it has all fifteen rounds in the magazine.

"Talib!" I say. "Put your weapon down!"

I want Burke to know I'm here. That he wasn't wrong.

That we're going to save those kids, bring down Talib and get out of this, together.

The house still reeks of sulfur and grime, and for the life of me

I can't figure out why Talib would bring his children here.

And then, as I'm trying to make out Talib, who is crouching in the space behind the stove in the darkened room, made out just by the hint of moonlight, Burke's words rise in my memory about Hassan's gang making meth in one of these abandoned houses in the Powderhorn area.

In 1997, drug cooks have switched from ephedrine pills to the unregulated pseudo-ephedrine pills. Only problem is they need to break it down to remove the key ingredient, which means added chemicals.

During the late '90s, we saw a sixty percent increase in meth-related home explosions, and memory lane has activated my sniffer.

We never ascertained the source of this explosion. Firefighters suggested a gas leak, and maybe a squatter fire, but you remember the smell drifting up from the basement, right?

What if Talib is cooking meth down in the bowels of 17th Avenue?

Maybe a spark ignites the combustibles he has stored in the basement.

We need to get out of here now.

"Rem!"

The voice shoots ice into my veins because *she is not supposed to be here.*

"Eve!" I see her, just outside the wedged door I came through. "What are you doing here?" You can imagine my panic, but I manage to keep my voice low.

She's crouched low in the darkness, her voice a rasp. "I'm with Shelby. We thought you might need help. So—here we are."

I stifle a word. "Eve, you need to go back to the car."

"Shelby is by the front door. And, she brought the radios."

Girl Scout that she is. "Pass it here."

Eve slides it along the floor, and I grab it. "Shelby?"

Her voice comes through the line, and I turn down the volume. "I'm here."

"Okay, listen to me. Danny's hurt. He's on the steps. I need you to get him out as soon as Burke and I take down Talib."

Because I've put it together.

In the first version of this nightmare, Burke and Danny had Talib pinned down. And then the house exploded. My guess is that Danny couldn't escape—not with his leg injury.

And Burke was burned. Probably trying to save Danny's life, if I know Burke.

Shelby confirms my request.

"Are the kids here?" Eve says, still by the door, and I'm starting to believe she can read my mind.

"Upstairs, maybe." But I don't know. Is time on my side? "There is a stairway, just behind me."

Another gunshot, and this time it's directed back at me. It chips off more wood and Eve stifles a sound as she gets down.

I hate to think of her in that pretty dress, getting it grimy.

I hate to think of her wounded and dying in my arms.

"Are you okay?" I hiss. "You need to get out of here."

"I'll get the kids—"

"No!"

Because it would be exactly fate's joke for Eve to be upstairs when the house explodes.

And there's no going back in time to stop it, is there?

"Please, Eve," I say. "*Please* go back to the car."

"Listen, Rem." Her voice is low in the darkness. "You're not the only one who wishes she could do things differently. I had someone who died, too. And if I could have saved her, I would have. I'm not going to let a couple kids die on my watch—"

"And I'm not going to let *you* die."

"It's not up to you," she snaps, and, *please, God!*

I know my wife. She doesn't take well to my telling her how to run her life.

"Please, Eve."

"Cover me," she says and slips into the back porch.

What am I going to do? This isn't a movie. I can't lay down fire. So I grab her and pull her hard behind me.

She hunkers down, breathing hard.

"Just stay down," I snap.

"Rem—the kids!"

"Stay. *Down.*"

Talib, in shadow, stands up. "Leave me alone!" he shouts and fires a couple more shots at Burke's position, then at me.

I lean away as the rounds chip off wood in the wall behind me, put my body between Eve and the bullets.

"You're shaking," she says.

I don't know where to start. Because you see it, don't you? The way that fate mocks me? All the pieces of my life are here, right *here* in this house that is swimming with poison, waiting to explode.

My father was right. I control nothing.

"I'm going up these stairs and getting the kids," she says. She's talking about the back stairs, and I'm pretty sure that Talib can't see her, but what if the kids aren't there?

What if she gets trapped?

"Talib!" Burke yells. "Let this be over."

"You get Talib. Shelby will cover Burke and my dad."

Of course. Her father. I'm not the only one she's here for.

"Eve—"

Before I can stop her, she's gone, just like that, slipping out of my grip, disappearing into the night, her feet pounding up the steps.

Another shot breaks a pane of glass beside me, and I cover up, to avoid being cut.

But Burke has returned fire, and really, I'm running out of time.

Then I hear a sound I don't expect. A grunt from across the room, the kind of grunt that means I've found home with one of my boilermakers.

Burke is hit.

And like I said, all the pieces of my life are in this house. I haven't glanced at my watch, but you feel it, too, right? The too-fast tick of time?

The terrible inhale before my life explodes.

Not this go-round.

Choices.

I roll into the room, hit my knees, aim and pull the trigger.

I hit Talib center mass.

He jerks, and then, just like that, he's down.

A beat, and I realize I've won.

Maybe—*please!*

Then I get up, and run toward Burke, find him on the floor, writhing.

He's shot, and it's bad, a gut shot bleeding hard into the floorboards. I know because Shelby has come running in, shining her light on Burke. I pull my gloves from my pocket and press it over the wound, but it's hopeless to stop the flow. "Call 911!"

But Shelby has run past me to the stairway where she's yelling. "Detective Mulligan. Wake up!"

His leg wound. Danny has been really quiet and while I try and staunch the blood from Burke's wound, I look up to see Shelby taking off the belt from her coat and wrapping it around Danny's leg. "Hang with me, sir," she's saying.

He's groaning, and we're all in big trouble here.

Especially since we're not alone.

Lights from the back, and I hear a voice I have tried to forget.

"Thought you could run from me, didn't you, Stone?"

I freeze and turn.

And Hassan Abdilhali has a gun leveled at me. I recognize him in the light that Shelby has shone toward the family room. He's wearing a leather jacket, his eyes white and I can barely make out his features in the wan light, but I know him.

I've spent years trying to nail him for a crime. *Any* crime.

Sadly, my death might be only crime I bear witness to.

"Hands up."

I put one hand up, because, you know the other is holding Burke's wound.

I can smell it now. The seepage of sulfur from the basement. The meth lab, I'm sure of it now.

It occurs to me that he's standing right around the place where Danny and I nearly fell through.

"Get up."

"I can't. My partner is down—"

"Maybe you watch him die, like I did my kid brother."

Right. Although Hassan didn't watch his brother die.

I did.

And it occurs to me that maybe this is a trap. An ambush for me, and Danny, and poor Burke got caught in the middle of it. I'm not sure, but, well, fate, right?

Danny and Burke have gone quiet.

I'm staring at Hassan. "What are you waiting for?" I say. "Because there's no time like right now."

The shot explodes from the stairwell.

Shelby drops Hassan, right there in the family room. The bullet tunnels through him, a gut shot that spills gore around the room..

The force of his body splinters the floor, and suddenly he's falling, shouting—so not quite dead yet.

I pick up Burke, haul him over my shoulder and make for the door. Shelby is behind me, Danny's arm over her shoulder, and she's dragging him.

Hassan is screaming, shooting from the bowels of the basement as we reach the door.

I don't know how I know it, deep in my gut—okay, call it a hunch, a *real* hunch, but the second I get outside, I simply launch us off the porch and into the snow.

The house explodes.

Fire blasts through the lower level of the house, blowing out the front windows and as I land in the snow, I cover up Burke, his body, his face, heat burning my jacket.

The flame dies back, but thunders as it consumes the house.

Nearby, Shelby has dragged Danny to the curb and is also huddled over him, although he has his arm around her, too.

Sirens whine in the distance—maybe Shelby got a call off.

I lean up, and Burke is staring at me. "What did you do?"

"I just saved your stinking life, partner."

He is groggy and groaning as I pack his wound with snow. And then—

Wait.

Where's Eve? *"Eve!"*

I stand up and look toward the house. It's an inferno, the flames shooting out the lower windows, licking out of the upper windows. Black smoke billows out of top floor.

And then I hear a voice.

Screaming my name.

I back up, my heart in my throat because I knew it.

I just *knew* it.

Time won't let me escape that easily.

Eve is on the top floor, shouting.

Trapped.

I see her scarf, the one I wrapped around her neck tonight when I took her to dinner.

When I stole her freakin' life from her.

No. The word is a groan inside me, even before I get up.

Burke has my jacket. "No!"

"Eve is up there!" I grab his hand but he's vised my lapel, despite his injury.

"No, man. You can't go in there."

"Like hell I can't!" I try to tear his fist away, but I can't so, of course, I turn, my eyes wide. "Don't make me hit you."

"Rem, you'll die!" Burke's eyes are red with fury, and if he weren't shot, I have a feeling history would repeat itself with a brawl. But he *is* injured and weak and in pain and *Eve is screaming*.

So, am I. "She's my wife, man! My *wife*!"

And I hit him.

He lets go and I turn, but the flames are roaring out the door. God, no!

I am not letting go.

My feet are moving, heading toward the back of the house, and please God, let there be a way up.

The back porch is not in flames, and I clamber onto it, and open the door.

The kitchen is burning, the flames crawling up the walls, into the ceiling, and smoke hazes the building.

I pull my scarf over my face and run to the stairs.

It's away from the fire, just enough, and I scramble up the first flight, then to the attic, dodging flames that are flickering along the edges of the floorboards. The smoke is so thick I hold my breath, but my eyes smart.

Eve is sitting near the open window, two children under her arms. They clutch her like she might be their mother. A little boy in pants and a puffy jacket, and a girl in a dress, pants, boots, a long jacket.

They're both screaming.

I hit my knees and grab Eve's jacket. "Eve!"

Her makeup is smudged as she looks up.

"Sorry Rem. I heard the shooting, and I should have come back downstairs! But now we're trapped—"

"C'mon, we can go down the stairs!" I pick up the little girl and take off across the attic, the fire now roaring.

But when I reach the stairs, they're engulfed, the flames shooting up to chew at our escape.

"Back to the window!"

I push Eve back, holding the little girl. Hadassah, right? And Ahmed?

Then I shove them into her arms. "Hide your faces."

I kick out the window.

Which, of course, is the wrong thing because the air swoops flames into the room. They crawl up the sides and into the rafters, gnawing at the air in the room.

Black smoke billows out of the window, around our heads.

I hunker down over Eve and the kids and pull them all close, my head down covering theirs and try not to weep.

"I'm sorry, Eve," I say quietly, my voice hiccupping. "I'm sorry."

Because in my quest to change time, I have killed us.

CHAPTER 18

Eve couldn't breathe. And not just because of the smoke that thickened the room, stealing the slightest sip of air, but with her stupidity.

Her thought that Rembrandt Stone might need her help.

For a second, her fight with Shelby—although, not much of one, given the fact that Shelby agreed with her—flashed through her mind.

"We should go with him." Eve had said it as she waited for the coat checker to hand out her coat, as Shelby zipped up her own, glancing out the door as Rem pulled out of the parking lot.

Shelby had looked at her, agreement in her eyes. "I was thinking the same thing. But he wants me to drive you home."

"I don't care what he wants. You saw him—clearly he thinks Burke's in trouble."

Shelby had sighed then and nodded. "That's the thing. I know what Burke says, but there's something about Rem's hunches." She paused. "I believe him."

That had settled it, right then. "C'mon," Eve had said. And no, she wasn't exactly attired for sneak and assault, nor was she armed, but it didn't stop her from finding Rem in the darkness.

From scooting in behind him. From pressing her hand to his chest, feeling his thundering heartbeat, the way he shook, just a little, probably from the hot adrenaline of being shot at.

"I'll go up these stairs, see if I can get the kids."

Oh, her stupid bright ideas. And she knew he'd try and stop her so, of course, she simply ran for it.

Up the stairs, to the second floor. The shooting downstairs kept her focused and she ran to each room, scanning it.

No kids. She took the stairs to the top floor.

The children huddled in a corner, their arms around each other.

Rembrandt, as usual, was right.

She'd grabbed them up, ready to run back down when another shot stopped her. Maybe she should wait until Rembrandt secured the shooter.

"C'mon, kids." She led them over to the window. Outside, sirens whined, and she closed her eyes.

Didn't Rembrandt say that her father was in the house? *Please, Daddy, be okay.*

But he would be. He was just as tough as Rembrandt. In fact, what had Burke said was true, *"Your father never stops working. He reminds me of Rembrandt."*

Yes, her father and Rembrandt were terribly alike, and that thought shook her, even as she held the kids.

Passionate, driven.

Committed.

"What's your name?" She asked the boy.

"Ahmed," he whispered. "And this is Hadassah."

"Are you okay?"

He nodded. She could barely make him out, save for his dark

eyes against white, the moonlight dim on his young face. He gave her a brave look, something that suggested he'd been trying not to cry.

"We're going to be okay," she whispered. "I promise."

And that's when her promises exploded.

Just like that, the floor convulsed under her, then shuddered as fire roared through the bones of the house.

She screamed. Brave Ahmed put his hands over his head, and Hadassah launched herself at Eve.

Fire ripped through the front windows, out into the street and she caught sight of Shelby on the lawn in the glow of the flames.

She tugged open the window, but it was stuck. Raking off her scarf, she shoved her arm through the space and let the scarf flutter. "Help!"

They were going to die if she didn't get the kids out of here. "C'mon!" She grabbed their hands.

Ahmed refused to move. "No—no—he's down there!"

He...Talib?

"No, he's not. My partner—" Yes. Rembrandt was her partner. Maybe not like Shelby was his partner, but the kind of team where they counted on each other.

Danced together.

At least she wanted to be.

"My partner arrested him. He's not going to hurt you."

But Ahmed had grabbed his sister, put his arms around her, shaking his head.

She crouched beside him, not sure if she could bodily carry him from the house. So she gathered them to her chest.

"Eve!"

The voice exploded through the room, right past the terror in her heart, and she looked up just as Rem skidded toward her on his knees.

Rembrandt.

And, *of course* he'd come for her.

His expression could terrify her if she knew it wasn't directed at her, at the fierce determination to get them out of this. His eyes watered, and smoke darkened his face.

"Sorry Rem. I heard the shooting, and I should have come back downstairs! But now we're trapped—"

"C'mon, we can go down the stairs!" He didn't even stop to consider—just picked up Hadassah and headed toward the stairs.

She had a grip on Ahmed's hand, pulling him up when—

"Back to the window!"

Rem had turned, and now pushed the little girl into her arms. "Hide your faces."

What?

He kicked out the window.

No—she wanted to scream at him—*that'll just suck the fire into the room*—

The flames whooshed up the stairs, crawling up the walls, into the ceiling.

She couldn't help the scream that lifted. Even when Rem hunkered down around them. His voice came out choppy, thick with emotion.

"I'm sorry, Eve, I'm sorry."

What? "Rem, this is not your fault—"

But he was shaking his head, tears cutting down his face, probably from the smoke, but even as he looked at her, those blue eyes in hers, she knew.

She'd fallen for this man. And whatever happened after this moment, she wasn't letting him go.

Yes, he was like her father. Which meant that sometimes he

was focused on a case and would disappear inside himself to solve it.

But clearly, when she needed him, Rembrandt showed up.

She reached out and grabbed his lapel, gripping it. "Rem—I—"

Water rushed in over them, flooding the room even as Rembrandt bent over them, pulling them down.

What—?

"Get them out!" Not Rembrandt's voice, but he responded by grabbing Hadassah and shoving her toward the window.

Eve looked up, and through the haze made out a fireman, pulling Hadassah to safety.

Then Ahmed.

"Eve, go—" Rem said. The burst of water the fireman had added to the room had evaporated, the flames roaring back behind him. His face lit with the blaze, so much intensity in it she felt it through his entire body.

Then his hands were on her, lifting her, propelling her through the window out into the frigid, clear air. She coughed even as the fireman pulled her into his arms onto the ladder. "Can you climb down?"

"Yes! Get Rembrandt!"

She started down, another firefighter below her as she went, but she looked up, and for a second, couldn't move.

The flames reached into the night, engulfing the house, and water from the hoses of two trucks sprayed the nearby houses, as well as arched over her. It fell upon her hair and coat, saturating her.

Firemen were shouting, but the fury drowned their voices.

The flames broke through the top of the roof, leaping through like tongues.

Rembrandt was still inside.

"Get him out!"

"C'mon, ma'am," shouted the fireman from below. "Hurry!" She felt his hand on her foot.

No—please—

Then, a form tumbled out of the window, gripping the ladder, coughing.

The fireman grabbed him by the jacket, held him steady on the rungs. But the house was going to implode if they didn't get down, so she put her head down and nearly fell getting down the ladder.

She collapsed in the snow, crawling away, the fireman's hands under her arms.

Not far from her, an EMT had her father on a gurney. "Dad!"

Shelby was holding the kids, staring at the house, the flames flickering on her face.

A couple more EMTs crouched over Burke, one of them packing a wound in his gut.

Shouting made her look up.

The front wall of the house was disintegrating, with the fireman and Rembrandt half way down the ladder.

"Jump!" She didn't know who shouted it—maybe her—but as the ladder fell, so did the men on it.

Rembrandt landed in the snow, some ten feet from the house. And didn't move.

No! Eve shrugged off the fireman's grip, launching herself toward him, sinking in the drifts, then crawling through the snow. "Rembrandt!"

He was rising to his hands and knees when she reached him. She grabbed his arm.

"Are you okay?"

He was breathing hard. His hair stuck out, singed, and his

jacket burned with holes from ash and embers. But he nodded even as he knelt before her and took her face in his hands.

He stared at her, his gaze roaming her face, as if drinking her in. "I can't lose you," he said, his voice shuddering. "I tried, but I can't...I can't let you go."

"You won't lose me," she said, gripping his wrists. "I'm not going anywhere, no matter what happens."

And she didn't know why, but something seemed to click in his expression, a sort of peace, maybe. Or resolution.

"Eve. I can tell you that...I'm not always myself. I know I can be a real jerk. But that jerk loves you. The guy who thinks he's invincible, who is obsessed and intense and a workaholic and sometimes forgets the people around him—that guy loves you, even if he sometimes forgets it. You have to know that."

She blinked at him. He *loved* her?

"So, believe me when the other guy shows up, okay? Because I'll be back. The *real me* will be back. And I'm not letting you go, either."

And then he kissed her, and he tasted of fire and blood and fear and the all-out fierceness that was the man she couldn't extinguish from her heart. And she didn't care that she was standing in the snow, starting to shiver with the cold pressing into her legs. Or that tomorrow he'd be risking his life again.

She loved this man, at least in this moment. And maybe, someday, beyond.

He drew away from her, his blue eyes holding hers, his breath trembling. Then he swallowed, closed his eyes, wincing. Pressed a hand to his ear.

"Oh no," he whispered.

"Rem? What is it?"

He opened his eyes, something urgent in his expression.

"Check on Burke. Make sure he's okay. And…stay away from Fitzgerald—"

"What's going on—"

"Promise me, Eve!" He gripped her arms, as if hanging on.

"You're scaring me."

"Promise—oh God—"

Then he ducked his head, gritting his teeth.

"Rembrandt!" She grabbed his wrists even as his hands fell from her arms. "Help! I think—"

He looked up at her, breathing hard, his gaze distant, as if searching for something. Finally landed on her. "Eve."

She stilled, not sure— "Are you…what just happened?"

He said nothing for a moment, looked behind him, at the burning house. At the fireman now shouting at them to get back. At Burke—she saw him now, being loaded into an ambulance.

"Burke? Is he okay?"

"He will be, I think," she said, frowning.

Now, finally, he looked at her. "You're a mess."

She frowned at him, then looked at herself. Yes. She'd ripped her hosiery, her jacket was filthy, and who knew what she looked like.

"Says the man with singed eyebrows."

He smiled, and it was a half-way, wry grin. "Yeah?" He touched his eyebrows. "But we got them, right? Talib, and Hassan?"

"Yeah. We got them."

He got up, then leaned down and pulled her up, too. Met her eyes with his. "Wow, you're pretty. I can't figure out why you keep showing up in my life, but…I like it."

Huh. Then he kissed her. Not like he had before, giving over a piece of himself, but this time something short, and yet young and vibrant and giving out the piece of him that suggested he was invincible.

The other guy.

Then he let her go, grinned at her, and headed through the snow to check on Burke.

He loved her.

Huh.

She made her way to the ambulance where they were loading in her father. Stood at the door. "Dad?"

He wore an oxygen mask, an IV inserted into his arm and lay on a gurney, a blood-soaked bandage around his leg, a tourniquet made from a coat belt around his upper leg. "What happened?"

"He was shot," Shelby said, coming up to her.

"And you saved his life," Eve said.

"I just did what Rembrandt told me to do."

Danny stirred, then leaned up, despite a shout from the EMT. Tore his mask to one side. "I was right about you," he said to Shelby. Then, "And Rembrandt." He looked at Eve, nodded.

"I'm riding with him," Eve said, getting in.

"Who are you?"

She looked at the man on the gurney. "I'm his daughter."

CHAPTER 19

The first thing I hear is laughter. It's deep and throaty and I'm trying to place it but it's just outside my reach.

Maybe it's Asher. Yes. He just left me, having delivered the watch.

I'm on my hands and knees on the floor, having caught myself in the fall through time, and there might be a scream in my head, too, because I had Eve in my arms, holding onto her.

And now, my hands are empty.

I sit back and run a trembling hand across my mouth, catching any remaining moisture.

Time coming at you, picking you up to carry you back always takes your breath away, hiccups your heart, runs a finger of terror through you to your spine.

My breath is shaky, but I push myself to my feet.

I'm in my office, and by the looks of it, I've changed nothing. Awards still clutter the shelves, and my screen saver is spinning.

I wiggle the mouse.

It opens to a Word doc, a half-typed paragraph.

Butcher found Jenny leaning over her microscope, her eye pressed to the lens, a dozen micro-slides lined up beside her.

"Any luck?"

"You'd better have coffee when you slink in this late," she said, not looking up.

I stare at it because, you know, I *finished* that novel.

"How's the writing going?"

The voice slips through me like a hot poker, jerking my head up.

Eve stands at the door. She's wearing a pair of jeans, a white dress shirt, her kinky auburn hair back in a ponytail.

I stand up, staring at her, because you know how it goes. What is she doing here? And…

I'm too afraid to hope.

"Does Butcher finally ask Jenny out?" She walks in and sits down on my leather chair.

My inspirational leather chair she gifted me, once upon a couple lifetimes. I stare it, at her, and my hope has a vice grip on my chest.

Please.

"I think so," I say.

"Who knew you were such a romantic," she says. "I thought Burke was the only romantic one of you two."

Burke. No, please no—and my heart sinks.

But the fact that Eve is here suggests maybe he doesn't hate me, at least.

"Dinner's ready, by the way. Asher is pulling the steaks off the grill."

Right. I still have a roommate.

Really, what did I expect?

She leaves and I follow her out of the office into the hallway.

Nothing looks changed. I'm still in my pre-remodeled crafts-man, with my bachelor furniture, a leather sectional, a big screen television. Me and the big fish.

I walk into the kitchen and see movement on the deck, the grill peeling off smoke, which Asher is trying to fan away with his spatula. He is in nearly the same attire as when I left— a pair of jeans, a T-shirt—and I'm starting to wonder if I *did* leave.

Briana is back, too, sitting on the deck sofa, wearing those short shorts and grinning at Asher like he is witty and charming.

But what really nabs my attention is Burke.

He's not burned. He's whole and handsome and strong and is smiling.

He sits at the table cradling a cold beer, droplets of conden-sation dripping down the dark bottle, his thumb running over the neck as he listens to whatever story Asher is telling.

He made it.

The back door opens, and my breath stills as Shelby leans in. She's wearing a pair of jeans and a T-shirt, still looking spectacular, although maybe not as tanned. "Rembrandt, can you grab the sal-ad in the fridge?"

Right. Clearly, we're together. And I'm trying not to let it show on my face.

Frankly, she's earned my trust after our last op, and maybe we are partners, if not on the job, then in life. Can I live with that? I'm not sure as I open the refrigerator and find a salad covered with plastic wrap.

I'm relieved, too, to see a couple beers and a half-wrapped sandwich from Dayton's Deli.

It looks like it might be ham salad, and my heartbeat slows as

I reach for the salad.

"I got it, Rem."

The voice turns me, and Eve is walking into the room. Where she went, I don't know, but she looks at me with so much warmth in her expression I stand there dumbly and hand her the salad.

She takes it and closes the fridge, then sets the salad on the counter. Her voice lowers, turns solemn. "So, what do you think of the good news?"

Oh no. "I don't know what to think…"

Then she takes my hand. "Rembrandt. This is a good thing. Yes, things will change, but you've been working toward this your whole life."

My whole life?

Right.

"Really, you two. We're hungry." Shelby has come all the way inside. "And Asher is pulling the burgers off the grill."

Shelby is pregnant. Her baby bump is showing under a T-shirt and around a flannel shirt that she wears open, over yoga pants.

My stomach drops because you know what I'm thinking.

Is this baby mine?

Maybe I go pale because Eve bursts out laughing. "Rem. You can't look so shocked every time you see Shelby. You and Burke— you act like you've never seen a pregnant woman."

Shelby runs a hand over belly. "A pregnant Chief of Police."

Eve laughs, "Right."

Shelby is *Chief of Police.*

"Although, not for long. Only two more weeks until Rem takes the helm."

I take the *helm?*

Which makes me…what? Deputy?

Shelby picks up the salad. "Hurry up, you too. The burgers are ready." She steps back outside.

"Are you okay?" Eve is looking at me, her face serious.

"I…I don't know." Because, I don't think I am. Any child I have, I want to be with her.

Eve laughs and touches my arm. "You're going to be fantastic. And…probably it's for the best, right?"

"Mmmhmm," I say, but my chest is so tight I can't breathe.

She goes quiet. Looks out the window. "It's a girl."

It's a girl. And the fact that she's telling me this nudges me. If I'm the father, wouldn't I know this?

I look out the window. And that's when I see Burke pull Shelby onto his lap. He pushes back her hair and kisses her neck.

The relief that rushes through me nearly buckles my knees—I know, dramatic, but really, I'm weak.

It's *Burke's* baby. Or at least, I think so.

"They're going to name her Daphne, after Shelby's mom."

Daphne. So maybe fate has given me mercy. Maybe I haven't screwed up another life.

"I'm happy for them. Really."

It's Eve's tone that catches me and I look over at her. "Eve?"

Her eyes have filled, however, and now I'm panicking again. I wish time would give me a short orientation before it plunges me back into my realities. A preview trailer, perhaps. "What is it?"

She reaches up and wipes a hand across her cheek. "I know we need to be happy for them even though it's hard…." She gives me a sad smile.

Them. *We.* And I so want to reach out and pull her to me, I can't stop myself. *Why is it hard?*

She comes willingly, wrapping her arms around my waist.

"It'll work for us, you'll see." she says. And as I hold her, I remember the miscarriage she had before Ashley.

She pushes back from me. Wipes her face again. "By the way, I brought home Meggie Fox's file. We're running DNA that we found on her body—we got lucky with this one, Rem. She fought him. We might finally have a solid lead on the Jackson Killer."

I still. What? I press my hands to my mouth, holding back a word because, really? We still haven't found Fitzgerald?

Oh, Meggie, I'm sorry. I hate that fate did this to Art, again.

Eve opens the fridge and pulls out a plate of cut vegetables for the burgers—tomatoes, pickles, onions, and lettuce. Closes it. Turns back to me. "Thirty-eight women." She shakes her head. "It's time to stop him."

Yes. Yes it is.

I walk out onto the deck. The sun is low, casting shadow into the yard, And I notice the giant dead elm at the back of the property, the one I took down in a previous life, still stands. My boat is also still sitting nearby, under a tarp, so that's a win. But mowing is in my near future, the grass a virtual jungle.

No swing set. Yet.

Asher is plating the burgers and sets them on the table. "Dad called. He and Mom are still in Chicago waiting for Lucas's baby to be born. But he said Happy Anniversary, Shelby. Five years as Chief."

Five years as Chief. Burke lifts his glass. "I thought for sure Chief Mulligan was going to give the job to Rembrandt." He's grinning. "You know what a bromance those two had after they took down the Brotherhood."

We did? But hoo-yah. *Yeah* we did.

"Hey, I helped. I killed Hassan Abdilhali," Shelby says.

"That's right, you did, babe." Burke raises his glass higher. "To our well-decorated Minneapolis Police Chief."

I raise a glass, but my brain is scuffing over Burke's previous words.

Danny was Chief? I barely stop the question before it emerges. (see, I've gotten better at this.) So, um, "I can't remember, when did Booker…step down?"

And now I'm getting a look from Eve. "I'd hardly call being *murdered* stepping down." She is shaking her head. "Armed robbery. You guys were in the wrong place, wrong time."

Robbery? Not an ambushed bombing at his house?

"It happened so fast. One day he's the chief, the next, he's gone," Shelby said. She looks at me. "We thought we lost you, for a while there, too."

Me?

And Eve's giving me a soft look. "You scared me, good."

"Sorry." But they're starting to unnerve me.

"In a way, your obsession with finding Fitzgerald sort of saved you. Gave you a focus," Burke says. "You *are* going to find him, man."

Shelby makes a face. "Sometimes I go back to that night, you know, the fire?"

I nod, because yes, *hello,* I know.

"And I think—what if I had gone out to that bar and arrested him?"

"I know," Burke says picking at the label of his drink. "The guy is slippery. You and Booker were so close after you pulled his address off that girl. What was her name? Gretchen?"

"Anderson?" I say. Except, in my memory, we never found an address on her.

The only address I have is from the non-existent ambush.

"Yeah. Her body was barely cold, but you had a hunch Fitzgerald was good for it. Too bad we didn't get to him in time." Eve is smiling. "You and your crazy hunches. Just like Booker."

Just like Booker.

Shelby raises her lemonade. "To John Booker."

I join her, but my brain is reeling with the math.

Gretchen Anderson died a month after the fire.

Which means... "John Booker has been dead for nearly twenty years," I say. It's more of a whisper of horror.

"Hard to believe," Eve says and pulls me over to the bench by the table. "He really liked you, too. I remember him showing up at the ER after you nearly got beat up—"

"Which time?" Burke says, and laughs.

"Remember that watch he used to wear?" Eve says. "And yet he was never on time. I don't even think it worked."

Oh, it worked, I want to say.

But that's when I look down at my wrist, and my heart goes cold.

I'm not wearing the watch.

I take a breath, then get up. "I'll be right back." I go inside, down the hall to my office.

Maybe I dropped it. But I was wearing it at the fire, so...

I search the floor, under the desk, pushing the chair back, and a sweat has broken out down my spine.

"Rem, are you okay?" Eve is standing at the door. "Did you lose something?"

I'm breathing hard, and I'm aware that I just might be having a panic attack.

The watch is gone.

Maybe Booker died with it on his wrist.

Maybe it was destroyed in the fire.

I don't know what is different than before, but I know this—I don't have the watch.

I can't fix this.

But my life is reset, right? Almost.

I'm still a struggling novelist, but I clearly have my career.

I have my wife.

And maybe someday, if fate is kind, we'll have a daughter named Ashley.

This is enough, isn't it?

I put my hand to my wrist, feeling the emptiness there.

I can't fix this.

Worse, the truth thrums deep in my soul.

Leo Fitzgerald is not the true murderer of those women.

I am.

So, yeah, I've lost something…my last glimmer of hope.

The epic series continues with Rembrandt Stone in two months. Check out a sneak peek of book four. Join us in August for the next installment.

THE TRUE LIES OF REMBRANDT STONE

SET IN STONE

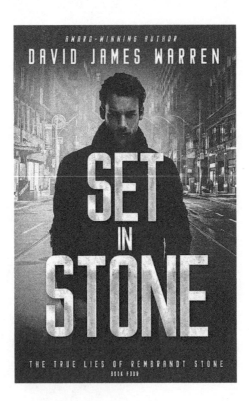

SET IN STONE - PROLOGUE

I can't live in this world. I won't.

I'm standing in the cool night, the mud and stink of the crime scene permeating my pants, my shirt, my skin. I'm cold—I'm sure of it—but I can't feel it.

I can't feel *anything*. No, the terrible howl of my soul has my full attention.

Around me, the local police are cordoning off the scene, running yellow tape between the open barn doors. I want to scream—it's not over yet! But words won't form.

No one looks at me. No one but Burke who stands a few feet away, keeping me in his periphery, glancing at me every thirty seconds, probably in case I do something crazy.

He's right, maybe, because it's not beyond me to charge back inside, push away the EMTs and do anything to bring her back.

Because if she's gone, it's over. Utterly, irrevocably, over.

I lift my eyes to the slate gray clouds and try to breathe.

My wrist is empty.

The girl I love is dead.

And I am stuck in time.

MEET
DAVID JAMES WARREN

Susan May Warren is the USA Today bestselling, Christy and RITA award–winning author of more than eighty novels whose compelling plots and unforgettable characters have won acclaim with readers and reviewers alike. The mother of four grown children, and married to her real-life hero for over 30 years, she loves travelling and telling stories about life, adventure and faith.

For exciting updates on her new releases, previous books, and more, visit her website at www.susanmaywarren.com.

James L. Rubart is 28 years old, but lives trapped inside an older man's body. He's the best-selling, Christy Hall of Fame author of ten novels and loves to send readers on mind-bending journeys they'll remember months after they finish one of his stories. He's dad to the two most outstanding sons on the planet and lives with his amazing wife on a small lake in eastern Washington.

More at http://jameslrubart.com/